Hula

Hula

a novel

Lisa Shea

W·W·Norton & Company

New York   London

Copyright © 1994 by Lisa Shea

All rights reserved

Printed in the United States of America

First Edition

The text of this book is composed in 12.5/16 Centaur,
with the display set in Centaur Bold Italic.
Composition by ComCom, Inc.
Manufacturing by The Maple-Vail Book Manufacturing Group.
Book design by Margaret M. Wagner.

Library of Congress Cataloging-in-Publication Data

Shea, Lisa.

Hula: a novel / Lisa Shea.

p.   cm.

1. Family—Virginia—Fiction.   I. Title.

PS3569.H39116H8   1994

813'.54—dc20   93-13144

ISBN 0-393-03589-1

W. W. Norton & Company, Inc., 500 Fifth Avenue, New York, N.Y. 10110

W. W. Norton & Company Ltd., 10 Coptic Street, London WC1A 1PU

1 2 3 4 5 6 7 8 9 0

For my sisters

With love to Alan, Jonathan, Francine, and Pavel. And with thanks to the MacDowell Colony, the Bread Loaf Writer's Conference, and the Word Girls. Thanks also to Carol and Amanda, Liz and Leigh; and to Mark, teacher after the fact. Lastly, love and thanks to my first loves, PAS and RMS.

The chapter "Pinks" appeared as a short story in slightly different form in *Columbia: A Magazine of Poetry and Prose.*

Nothing will catch you.
Nothing will let you go.

—From "Tennessee June"
by JORIE GRAHAM

Contents

11

Hula

Prologue:
A Good Enough Place
to Hide

In the summer in Virginia, the bricks of our house heat up so we can't lean against them if we're hiding out front in the blue hydrangea.

Instead, my sister and I hide in the forsythia bushes down by the ditch, or up in the mimosa tree or on the roof of the garage or behind the woodpile where the Vollmers' dogs get through the fence. Sometimes we crawl into the drainpipe that runs under the driveway. Things float in there when it rains popsicle sticks, bubble gum wrappers, the arms and legs and heads of dolls we've thrown in after torturing them.

Up in the pear tree that doesn't give pears, my sister and I tie the dolls with string and hang them from the branches. Then we whip them with the long, slender branches we've stripped from the forsythia bushes. After we're done, my sister cuts the dolls down with a knife.

Without their arms and legs and heads, the dolls look like our dog Mitelin's chew bones scattered in the tall, spiky grass. We rest under the tree for a while and then we bring the dolls down to the drainpipe and throw them in.

There are lots of other places to hide in the summer. In the blackberry bushes in the backyard where our rabbit Lily lost her tail. We found it stuck on a bramble. It never grew back. Now she licks and licks that spot with her leg shooting up out of her body like a missile.

Mitelin can find us even if we're hiding in a new place. We'll pull her in on top of us, with her big head lying across my chest, butting into my chin. To me she smells like the whole world—fur, flowers, smoke, grass, dirt.

When our father finds us, we have to march around the yard and then lie down on our bellies with our arms up over our heads. Sometimes he pretend-shoots us with his gun.

"You're dead, soldier," he says. I pretend I don't have any arms or legs or a head.

My mother says something happened to our father in the war but my sister says he is just mean. In the back of his head is a hole where no hair grows. Where no hair grows there is a metal plate attached to his head. In the sun, light strikes the metal plate like signals from a flying saucer.

Sometimes, our father hits his head with his fists.

Once, my sister and I hit our heads and we both saw stars. Other times he chases us up the stairs with his rope belt. By the time we get to the top, our legs are burning hot.

Our mother used to be a dancer. She taught the conga, tango, rumba, mambo, and cha-cha. She also taught the hula, the limbo, the dance of the seven veils. Now she works in a room above the studio, making costumes for the shows they put on.

When she met our father, she was dressed like a hula girl at a luau party and he was in charge of roasting the pig. She says our father's eyes were angry and blue and when he watched her hula, that was the end of her. She moves around in a little circle in the kitchen, doing one of the dances with the funny-sounding names. We watch, and my sister whacks the refrigerator over and over with the flyswatter until the handle breaks off.

When no one is home, we practice dancing in the living room. So far, my sister has taught me the twist, the hitchhiker, the watusi, and the swim. Sometimes we just bend and jump and twirl our bodies around. We call it the dance with no name because it can be anything.

Now we climb in through the punched-out windows of our father's burned-up car, parked on cinder blocks beside the driveway. Tall grass sticks up out of the engine. It pokes through the giant holes in the floorboards. My sister says our father blew the car up in an accident.

I tell her it might have burned up coming from outer space. She tells me to shut up about outer space.

From the backseat, we watch the sun go down. Birds fly off the telephone wires into the purple-and-orange sky. Our father pulls into the driveway in his new used car with the tied-on tailpipe that scrapes the ground. At night when he races down the driveway, we watch the sparks. Now he gets out of his car and walks past us toward the house. His shadow shoots up over the roof.

I ask my sister again if she thinks he's from outer space and she says No, but you are.

We stay in the backseat until it is almost dark and then we climb out of the car and walk up the driveway to our house. Slowly our shadows rise off the ground until they are smack against the bricks. Our shadows come up at us and then my sister pushes open the door and we go in.

Summer
1964

1

King and Queen

We are sitting on the front steps watching the storm come. The sky is getting dark and the air smells sharp and wet. I don't have any top on because we got chased out of the house by our father, who is arguing with our mother. Our father's voice is the thunder getting closer. Our mother's voice is the wind shaking the pointy leaves of the mimosa tree. There isn't any lightning yet. My sister looks at me and her eyes go down to my chest.

"Cover yourself," she says.

"I don't have anything."

"Your hands."

I put my hands over my chest. Leaves and petals and pieces of grass are flying in the air. Mitelin comes up from where she has been rooting in the ditch and sits with us. Her nose and paws are covered with ash. She tries to push her muzzle into my ribs but I twist away. I don't want the ash on me. The ash might be Jupiter, who got run over.

My sister covers her ears. From behind a cloud rimmed in green, lightning flashes.

"Heat lightning," says my sister, too loud.

"It might be real lightning," I tell her when she puts her hands down.

"Real lightning can kill you," she says.

Now the sky is blue-black and the rain is falling sideways. I hold on to Mitelin so she won't jump off the porch into the bushes. Lightning crackles over the houses and the trees, it flashes on our arms and legs and faces. Our skin glows.

Our mother opens the front door and tells us to take Mitelin and wait in her car.

"Mrs. Cooley's," says my sister.

Mrs. Cooley lives in the neighborhood across the highway. When we stay with her, we get to sleep on the pull-out couch in the living room. Mrs. Cooley says the only other people allowed to sleep on it are the King and Queen.

My sister loops her finger through Mitelin's choke collar and leads her down the steps into the rain. I wait until they are almost to the driveway and then run along the bushes in front of the house. The rain punches into my shoulders and back.

In the car, Mitelin jumps into the storage well behind

the backseat. She can sit in it and lie down but she can't stand up. I brush my hand on the steamed-up glass and there is the house, the bushes, the sidewalk, the trees. Rain is rushing down the driveway.

"This is the safest place in a lightning storm," my sister says. "Because of the tires."

"What about them?"

"Shut up," she tells me. "It's science."

"What about the King and Queen?" I ask her.

"Who?"

"At Mrs. Cooley's."

"There isn't any King and Queen," she says.

"There might be," I say, rubbing a new spot on the steamed-up window. I look out, thinking about who the King and Queen might be. The wind shakes the bushes and the trees. It yanks open the screen door and slams it back against the house.

The window steams up again but I don't wipe it clear.

My sister punches all the buttons on the radio, pretending to listen to different songs. A thunderclap breaks, rattling the car. Lightning flashes and crackles in the branches of the trees. Mitelin jumps from the well into the backseat. I try to grab her but she leaps up into the front seat next to my sister. She won't keep still.

"Are we going to die?" I ask my sister.

"I told you," she says. "Cars are safe."

Still, I saw her hand jump away from the radio knob.

Now her hands are folded under her arms. I try to push Mitelin down onto the seat but she keeps turning around and around.

"Mitelin!" my sister yells and yanks her into her lap. She strokes Mitelin's big, square head until Mitelin is asleep and her paws start to twitch.

"I'm going in," she says but she doesn't move.

Mitelin moans in her sleep and my sister and I laugh.

"She's chasing Lily," I say.

"No," says my sister. "She's with Aloysius."

Aloysius is our next-door neighbor's dog who Mitelin had puppies with. Once when they were mating, he and Mitelin got stuck together and our father had to turn the hose on them. When Aloysius finally let go, his penis was fiery red and hung down almost to the ground. He might be the King, and Mitelin could be the Queen.

My sister leans her head against the window and closes her eyes. Her eyeballs move like animals under her eyelids, like the puppies in Mitelin's belly did before they were born.

"Don't look at me," she says, without opening her eyes.

I keep looking.

The thunder and lightning have stopped, but it is still raining. I turn around in the seat and wipe a clean spot to look out the back window. The rain is rushing down the driveway, making a pool that is dark with ash from the ditch. Leaves and pieces of paper twirl in the black water.

Sometimes in a storm, our father stands in the doorway with his hands on his hips. We'll watch him from the top of the stairs, his head uncovered, his whole body lit by flashes, daring the lightning to hit him.

"Dad might be the King and Mom might be the Queen," I tell my sister, "and we might be the princesses."

"We're the prisoners," she says.

Mitelin pushes herself from my sister's lap to sit. The back of her head is smooth and flat. At the top is a bump the size of a marble. She has always had it, the way my sister has a space between her front teeth that she can stick a ruler in. On my right ankle is a scar that one day just appeared. My sister said I'll know soon enough if it's cancer.

The rain is coming down hard again, filling the wheelbarrow we left out near the mulberry tree, and the metal tub we wash Mitelin in and the bucket under the spigot near the side porch. I picture my mother inside the house, covering her face with her hands while our father punches his head with his fists.

I wish the King was my father. I wish the Queen was my mother.

I look out at the house. The red bricks have run black from the rain.

"How long do we have to wait?" I ask my sister.

"Until," says my sister.

"Until when?" I want to know.

"Until you shut up!" she yells.

Mitelin gets up and jumps into the backseat and pushes past me into the well.

"Stay!" I yell at her.

It is getting dark out and the rain has stopped. We sit in the car.

"I don't think we're going to Mrs. Cooley's," I tell my sister.

"And there isn't any stupid King and Queen," she says.

I don't answer right away, and then I say, "Okay."

Mitelin pushes herself up from her sleeping position in the well and then, because she can't move any other way, lies back down.

After a while, I reach for the back of my sister's blond ponytail and hold it. She doesn't tell me to let go, so I keep holding it while the night comes down around the house and the trees and bushes and the car.

g o r i l l a

In the middle of dinner, our father gets up to put on his gorilla mask and hands. He keeps them on the top shelf of the living-room closet, next to our mother's winter hats and gloves. After our father leaves the table, our mother tells us to keep eating. For dessert, she says, there will be watermelon and vanilla wafers.

I feed my hot dog to Mitelin, who is waiting under the table for scraps. After she lies back down, I take off my zories and rest my feet on her thick, smooth fur.

Our father comes in wearing his gorilla mask and hands, swinging his arms and beating his chest. My sister puts her hands over her plate. Our father pushes her hands away, grabs at her food and pokes sauerkraut through the mouth hole in his mask. He moves around the table, swiping food from the paper plates and guzzling from the cups. Near my mother he bangs his head on the knickknack shelf and one of the snow globes falls and breaks on the floor. It's the one with the satellite inside.

When our father comes near me, I slide down under

the table, but he pulls me back up by his hairy rubber hands. I don't say anything. He likes being the gorilla. After dinner, when he takes off the mask and hands, his face will be flushed and there will be tears in his eyes.

2

Hula

After my sister and I get the dogs into the hula skirts we sit with them in the shade in the front yard. It is cool there and the skirts match the color of the grass. All afternoon we have played with Mitelin and her son Max, who lives next door with Aloysius. We found homes for all the others except Jupiter, who got run over. Our father lifted him off the road with a shovel and brought him out back to the wire trash can. He put Jupiter in the trash can with some gasoline and papers and lit a match. We watched the flames go up and up until all that was left of Jupiter was thin triangles of red dark ash being sucked in and out by the wind.

Today we made leis from peonies and irises to go with the skirts. Mitelin is wearing my lei, plus we have fastened a blue hydrangea behind one of her ears. She lies back in the dark grass. Max chews at the waistband of his skirt covering him from his penis the size of a fingertip on down. So far our father hasn't found out about the skirts, which our mother brought home from the dance studio. He already took away the Scottish kilts and the Japanese kimonos. He says we don't need all that junk, except for the coolie hats from a show about the Far East, which he lets us wear when we work in the garden. He grows radishes and onions in there.

What I like about the hula skirts is how silky they feel, not like the grass over the sump pump in our back yard that is pointy and prickly and mostly weeds. When the pump overflows, the ground softens and swells. Once, my sister dared me to walk over it. Halfway, the sludge sucked at my shoes and pulled me down into what she says is the beginning of hell. She took a step to save me and fell in. The sludge went up around her ankles and wrists.

"I don't want to go to hell," I cried, and my sister said, "Too late."

Our father heard our screams and came up from the ditch where he was burning off dead leaves. He made us grab his fire stick, which was still hot, and pulled us out. At the top of the driveway he stood us back to back and turned the hose on all the way. We kept moving in circles but it wasn't like dancing. The water punched into us, spraying off our fronts and backs and faces. Turning, I saw the sunlight coming down through the branches of the mulberry tree and my mother leaving the porch to stand on the steps and my father's free hand, made into a fist as big as a yellow onion on his hip.

When he was finished, our father shut off the hose and dropped it in the driveway. He walked to the house and pushed by our mother going up the stairs.

Now there is a fence around the sump pump to keep us out, but Mitelin will go in there when the ground is dry and sniff around. She'll squat down, her square head high and her back legs shaking like she is having puppies.

It is getting dark now around the bushes in the front yard. When I think about what could be hiding in them, the muscles in the top of my head creep back. My whole body starts doing the dance with no name. My sister really can dance. She dances to Chubby Checker records in our bedroom with the door closed. I go in when she isn't there and look at all her things. Once, she caught me and beat me fifty times on the arm. I'm watching that place on my arm now for cancer.

The dogs start to move around. Mitelin's flower drops from behind her ear into the dark grass. Max sniffs at his mother's teats. They are still brown with milk but are slowly shrinking back to pink, flattening down into her body. We each grab one of the dogs and get them out of the hula skirts. We aren't supposed to pick any flowers, so I take Mitelin's lei apart and stomp it into smelly confetti.

We call the dogs in to the garage, where we stand on chairs and hide the skirts in the top of the broken player piano. After she closes the lid, my sister reaches into our father's army knapsack hanging from a hook above the piano. She pulls out his army pistol.

"A ray gun!" I shout.

"You wish," she says, looping her finger around the trigger and pointing the gun in the air. I tell her to put the gun back but she keeps waving it around. She points it at me saying Make your last wish and I jump down from the chair and run outside to the top of the driveway. Lily is hunched down under the purple azalea. The dogs come up from the ditch and run in circles around my legs. I look up at my parents' open bedroom window, at the torn white curtain being sucked out by the breeze. Behind me my sister pulls the garage door shut.

On practice day, we put on the leis we made from blue hydrangea, then we get the hula skirts out of the top of the broken player piano and bring them to the front yard. Mitelin and Max are down in the ditch. Our father burns weeds and dead leaves in there. Afterwards, when the ground is cool, the dogs go in and root. They come back up onto the lawn, their noses covered with ash. I push them away so the ash won't get on me but they keep coming back around, nudging into my chest and shoulders and arms. It is a game to them. To me it is work.

Now my sister puts on her hula skirt over her shorts. She begins to dance, pushing her arms out to one side and moving them in waves. Then she shimmies her hips so that her whole body is vibrating. I step into my skirt and pull it up around my waist. It is easy to move my arms but my hips won't shimmy.

"Don't think about it, just do it," says my sister.

I watch her, and then I start to sway my hips back and forth. My sister is still shimmying when our father's car comes up the driveway. She scrambles out of her hula skirt as fast as she can, her arms moving like crazy helicopter blades.

"Take yours off!" she yells, but I can't get my body to obey. My sister is gone. I want to be invisible but it is too late. My father rips the skirt off me, the rope belt burns into my waist.

After he goes inside, Mitelin comes out from under the forsythia bush to sniff around. I lie still in the grass until she comes close and then I pull her down on top of me.

On the day of the burning, my sister and I wait by the wire trash can. In it the hula skirts look like new grass.

Other things have been thrown in on top of the skirts: papers, weeds, small branches and twigs, leaves from the ditch. At the bottom of the trash can is a layer of ash. Jupiter must be way down past the ash by now or else he is way up in the air. After that, he could be anywhere.

Our father lights a match and tells us to step back. He holds the match to the gasoline-soaked papers deep inside the trash can and we watch the fire jump up. Mitelin and Max come up the slope but our father throws his arms up and calls them off. Mitelin heads back down the hill to the apple tree and Max follows her. She lies in the shade under the tree and Max drops down beside her.

When the flames get as high as the hula skirts, there is a whooshing noise and the green plastic grass curls up fast into the center of the fire. The skirts disappear inside the black smoke.

My father isn't watching the fire. He is looking across the fence into our neighbor's yard. Even though he's standing apart from us, his shadow stops just short of my feet. Slowly I move my foot until it is stepping on the part of his shadow that is his head. I put all my weight down on that foot.

After the burning, I walk down to where the dogs are lying under the apple tree. It is cool there and the air around the tree smells smoky sweet. Bees climb inside the fruit that we raked into piles on the ground. My sister calls to me from our bedroom window, but I pretend not to hear. I don't know where my father is. He has gone somewhere, into the garage or into the house. My mother could be anywhere.

I watch the dogs, thinking Mitelin still made the best hula girl, with her nut-brown color and her almond-shaped eyes. For the show, she would have let us hold her front paws while she dog-danced on her hind legs, the way she does when my sister plays her Chubby Checker records.

I lie down next to the dogs. The fire is practically burned out but I can still hear the embers squeaking and ticking. My sister calls me again. This time I look up. She is pointing the gun out our bedroom window. She keeps pointing it when our father comes out of the garage. My whole body begins to shake. Our father is moving toward the house. She follows him with the gun. He is on the stairs, reaching for the door. My sister leans a little further out the window with the gun. When our father pulls the door open, Max gets up but Mitelin growls and he lies back down. I shut my eyes and move closer to the dogs. From the bedroom window I hear a click.

After she puts the gun back in the garage, my sister finds me under the apple tree.

"There weren't any bullets," she says.

"I know."

"He took our skirts."

"Will you still teach me the hula?" I ask.

"Sure," says my sister.

We walk out to the top of the driveway where there is sun. She puts her arms out and starts to shake her hips.

"Stupid. Don't just watch me, you do it," she says.

I move my arms in waves and and then I try to shake my hips but it still feels like I'm doing the dance that has no name.

coolie

Today we are putting on a skit for the neighborhood. I play a Chinese coolie. It isn't a speaking part. My job is to water the plants while the people I work for gossip in their fancy garden. The talkers are played by my sister and her friend Deborah McDermott.

I have on Chinese pajamas and my straw coolie hat. We slanted our eyes and put red lipstick on our mouths and cheeks. We're charging twenty-five cents for kids and fifty cents for adults. With the money we're going to get new grass skirts for our hula show.

When all the people have been seated in the backyard, we start the play. I come out first, after my mother pushes me from behind the curtain pinned to the clothesline. I walk around the garden inspecting the flowers. When I see a plant that is dry, I pretend-water it with the watering can we got from the garage. Behind the curtain, my mother taps the metal washtub with a stick. This is the signal for my sister, Mrs. Ming, and her play sister, Mrs. Wong, to come out.

They are dressed like high-Chinese in long skirts and blouses with matching vests. Our mother made all the outfits from leftover costumes at the studio, and she braided and looped Mrs. Ming's and Mrs. Wong's hair. In the play, the sisters gossip about their husbands and their children, and about the husbands and the children of their friends. The sisters say anything they want to me, but I am not allowed to talk back. They even tell jokes, but I pretend not to hear. My job is to act invisible.

While Mrs. Ming and Mrs. Wong are talking, before the part where they get into an argument, I notice that the ground over the sump pump has started to swell. The shoes of some of the people at the end of the first row are getting wet. I make a bow to the sisters and walk behind the curtain to tell our mother.

At the intermission, we move all the chairs away from the ooze, but it keeps spreading into the second row. Some people leave. Our mother tells the audience she'll refund their money if they'll follow her out to the driveway. She takes the cash box and they file out slowly behind her. Mrs. Wong is crying. My sister, Mrs. Ming, is smacking the curtain with the gong stick. The strap of my coolie hat is pinching me under my chin.

After all the people leave, our mother finds us on the front porch, where we're sitting to get away from the smell. Nobody says anything about our father. He has been gone again for two days. When he comes back, I'll try to be invisible, but not my sister. She'll stick out like she usually does.

Deborah McDermott says she is going to throw up from the smell and our mother takes her inside.

My sister opens the cash box and counts the money.

"We'll never be hula girls," I say when she is finished counting two dollars and twenty-five cents.

"You can't even do the hula," she says, throwing the money back into the box.

We wait for Deborah McDermott. When she doesn't come back out, my sister says our mother probably sent her home.

"She's a crybaby, like you."

"I'm not a crybaby. I'm a coolie."

"You're my slave," says my sister.

We stay on the porch until the sun is a fiery orange ball on the horizon. Then my sister stands and lifts her skirt, delicately, high-Chinese style. She nods to me, barely moving her head, and I stand up and bow. She walks slowly into the house. I pick up my watering can and follow her inside, pretend-watering our footsteps as we climb the bright black stairs up to our room.

3

A Story from the War

When the gun goes off, my sister and I run to our bedroom window. Down below in the backyard our father is sitting with John Guidry. John Guidry has TB. Their shirts are hanging from the backs of their chairs and they are drinking beer out of green-and-gold cans. Our father is wearing his sun-shield hat, so the metal plate in his head doesn't heat up. On a cord hanging from his neck is his black scapula.

Both of the men have their guns out. Our father's gun is on the arm of his chair. John Guidry picks his up and starts waving it around as he talks. His arms are so thin I can see the blue veins. In the winter he sleeps on our living-room couch. Our mother tells us to stay upstairs, but we go down in the morning and listen to his noisy breathing.

I start to talk. My sister shushes me, keeping her face pressed to the screen.

We listen to the men. We know they're talking about the war, because their voices are excited. John Guidry tells our father again about how he found a gold-and-silver sword in the plantation house he and some other men captured. John Guidry slaps down his gun on the arm of his chair. He keeps talking, so long that his thin legs stiffen and he has to stand up out of his chair and then sit back down. He begins to cough again and doesn't stop until he has spat for a long time into his balled-up yellow handkerchief.

Our father hands John Guidry another beer and tells him about how he lived in the jungle after his company was ambushed. He talks about the men he killed in hand-to-hand combat, and how fast their bodies swelled in the heat. Our father picks up his gun and shoots the metal trash can at the back of the garage. He tells another story about huge snakes dropping at night from the trees. We wait for him to tell the story about the metal plate, but he never does.

The men keep telling stories from the war while the sun moves across the yard from the back porch to the tops of their heads to the apple tree and then up the hill to the woodpile. We keep watching, to see if they'll do any more shooting, but they just move their guns around as they talk and take sips of beer from the cans they keep in the grass at their feet.

Our father's face is bright red. John Guidry's face is pale white. My sister says he shot his way out of a sanatorium.

The sun keeps moving. The men shift in their chairs.

After a while, John Guidry gets up, and he sways on his legs, waving his gun, saying something to my father in a funny language.

"Japanese," says my sister.

"Is he drunk?" I ask.

"Watch the gun," she says.

He is still talking, waving the gun at the apple tree, the back of the house, the mulberry tree, the garage. Suddenly, our father jumps out of his chair and grabs John Guidry's gun away from him. He takes him to the back of the garage and makes him kneel down. Then he holds John Guidry's gun on him.

"What are they doing?" I whisper to my sister.

"Watch," says my sister.

Our father circles around John Guidry and then he puts one hand on John Guidry's shoulder and hits him on the back of the head with his gun. John Guidry slumps over onto his side. After that he doesn't move. My sister and I look at one another.

"Is he dead?" I ask.

"Maybe," she says, looking out the window again. I look, too. John Guidry is still lying on the ground but then he starts to cough, his head thrust forward and his whole body twisting wildly.

"The TB," says my sister.

Our father puts the gun in the waistband of his pants and bends over John Guidry to help him up. When he finally stops coughing, John Guidry gets out his yellow handkerchief and spits into it so many times I lose count. He's laughing, looking around for his beer. Our father walks him back to his chair.

"He only pretend-hit him," I tell my sister when the two men are sitting in their chairs again talking and drinking.

"I knew," says my sister.

John Guidry lights a cigarette and holds it between his fingers that look like sticks of chalk. He doesn't smoke the cigarette, it just burns, and the smoke streams off. After a while, he pulls another can of beer from the bag under his chair. In his shirt pocket is a can opener. He drinks the beer fast like it's soda.

The men keep talking and drinking, but after a while we can't understand what they're saying. It might be a secret code the way their heads nod slowly, the way their arms and legs barely move. Their beers tip over into the grass.

When John Guidry finally drops forward with his lit cigarette sticking out of his mouth, our father gets up out of his chair and pulls John Guidry to his feet. He knocks the cigarette away and steadies John Guidry by his side, holding on to him, and leads him out of the backyard.

"They drank twenty beers," my sister tells me after the men have disappeared down the driveway.

We look out the window at all the beer cans lying in the grass under and around their chairs. I start to count the cans but stop when I hear John Guidry's car drive away.

Our father comes back into the yard. His sun-shield hat is pushed way back on his head and his black scapula is twisted over his shoulder on its cord. He finds his gun under the seat cushion of his chair and shoots it into the grass. Then he shoots the apple tree and the side of the garage. He isn't aiming the gun. He is just pointing it and pulling the trigger. The bullets are going everywhere, into the soggy ground over the sump pump and near the hula hoops we left out overnight and near Mitelin's chain that is coiled like a shiny snake near the clothesline.

From the window, we watch him reload the gun. He shoots it into my sister's pumpkin that she grew from a pack of seeds.

"Look," I tell her. "Eyes."

"Shut up," she says.

Our father keeps shooting until there aren't any bullets left. He puts the gun in the waistband of his pants and walks over to the garage to look at the holes he has made there. With his finger he rubs around the openings and then he sticks his head close and with one eye looks in.

"I'm going down," my sister says.

I don't want to, but I follow her. At the bottom of the stairs, we stop and listen. We hear the tailpipe of our father's new used car scraping along the ground. Our mother isn't anywhere in the house.

Outside, my sister and I search around the men's chairs for whatever might have dropped out of their pockets. My sister looks inside the bag under John Guidry's chair and pulls out an unopened can of beer. She tells me to get her the can opener from the kitchen and after I bring it to her she opens the beer. I tell her not to drink it but she does anyway. When she finishes, her eyes are watering. I ask her what it tasted like but she won't tell me. She sits down in John Guidry's chair and leans back, holding her stomach like she is going to be sick.

"What if you get TB?"

"I'll cough on you," she says.

I sit in my father's chair. The damp, sweaty cushion feels cool on the backs of my legs. My sister's eyes are closed. The skin on her arms and the tops of her legs is covered with goose bumps. The sun is past the black-berry bushes, past the woods.

Mitelin has crawled underneath the sump pump fence and is sniffing the spiky grass. She looks up at us and her black eyes shine. When my sister is asleep I pick up the tipped-over beer can and lick the opening until the salty taste of the warm liquid comes into my mouth.

Two policemen come into our backyard and I wake my sister up. They ask us who lives here and we say we do. They ask us who else lives here and we say our mother and father but they aren't home right now. Then the police ask us if we heard any gunshots in the last two or three hours and we say no. They say someone in the neighborhood reported hearing gunshots coming from our backyard and my sister says it was boys setting off fireworks. The policemen look around our yard. They ask us if our mother or father own any firearms and we look at them like what are those. One of the policemen sees the can of beer on the grass and says You girls are a little young to be drinking beer and my sister says the boys with the firecrackers left it here.

After the policemen leave, my sister and I go hunting for bullet holes. The one we both saw in the side of the garage doesn't count. She smashes her pumpkin open

with a cinder block and I run to the apple tree. The bark
is split and smells like gunpowder. You don't have to
find the bullet, only the bullet hole.

My sister checks the pieces of her pumpkin. I look
around the hula hoops and Mitelin's chain.

We search around the back of the garage. My sister is
the first to find a bullet hole, in the metal trash can filled
with ashes for the garden. Where the bullet went in, ash
has spilled. My sister picks up a handful and sifts it
through her fingers.

"Jupiter," I tell her.

"Jupiter is in the ground," my sister says.

"He might be in the air."

"He went down," she says.

She throws the ash away. I close my eyes so a speck
won't fly in. It might be Jupiter.

It's getting too dark to hunt for bullet holes. In the
box we keep in our dresser, there are two real bullets.
The box is lined with red velvet that we decorated with
silver and gold stars. At night, when you open the box,
the stars shine down on the bullets. My sister says she
found both bullets, but I know she took them from our
father. He keeps them in the basement closet under the
stairs, where white spiders hang upside down from the
ceiling.

My sister's pumpkin is still lying in pieces in the grass.
It smells like the sump pump when it overflows. She

starts kicking the pieces around, kicks them until her pumpkin is all over the yard, bits of orange in the grass everywhere. When she is finished, I pick up some of the pieces, but my sister flies at me and slaps them out of my hands.

"We'd better go in," I say, but my sister steps away in the dark. She keeps moving away into the night that is going everywhere now, around the house and the clothesline and the bushes and the garage and the trees. I walk slowly toward the house. Lily runs in front of me and disappears into the bushes.

One of the stars has fallen off the lining of the bullet box. We find it in the bottom of the dresser drawer in our room and my sister sticks it back on with her spit.

"I'm getting a gun," she says.

"How can you?"

"Steal it."

"That's a sin."

"Not when it's a war," says my sister.

She stands up and puts the box back in the dresser drawer. If I had a gun, I would chase my sister under her bed with it and not let her come out.

"You can't get a real gun," I tell her when she is lying back on her bed.

"I'll get a gun," she says.

The house is quiet except for the sound of our mother downstairs ironing. When she sets the iron upright on the ironing board, the steam hisses out like a sigh.

I call to my sister but she is already asleep. She says she has dreams about being in the war, everybody shooting guns and speaking different languages. I close my eyes and try falling asleep, but my eyes keeping popping back open, like anything could happen if I close them, anything at all.

bluebird

In the forsythia bushes, my sister's hand moves like a bird hop-flying from limb to limb. She is in there by herself because she got yelled at for cutting open the pineapple our father brought home from the supermarket. He's the only one who can cut into or open anything new. Once I opened a carton of ice cream and ate some. Instead of putting the carton back, I left it out by the trash can for Mitelin. After she finished licking the ice cream, her chops were milky white. I took the carton to the edge of our yard and flung it into the blackberry bushes.

My sister pretends not to see me. She keeps moving her hand like a bird, flitting it along the branches. When she turns her head to look away from me, her ponytail snags on a branch. The part that isn't caught falls in a spray past her shoulders.

"I'm stuck," she says.

I reach my hand through and free her ponytail, holding it for an extra few seconds before I let go, feeling its silky thickness. My sister tells me to leave but I don't. She loops her ponytail around her finger and then pinches it up through the rubber band so it stays tight in a bun at the back of her head. This makes her look much older. It makes me want to kiss her.

A cardinal lands on a branch above our heads. It is deep red and has a pointed crown—a male. My sister shakes the branch—hard—and the bird flies away. We watch him land in the mimosa tree. The thin branch bobs under his weight. He pecks at a blossom until it falls.

"That's me," my sister says.

"I'd be a bluebird," I tell her.

"You'd be a crow, a scaredy-crow," she says. She is smiling.

"I'd eat you," I say.

"I'd peck a hole in your stomach and get out."

My sister watches the cardinal. She mimics him, turning her head in quick, sharp movements.

"He's looking for his mate," I say.

"Maybe she died," says my sister.

"I don't think she died," I say.

We watch the bird. When the back door slams, my sister pulls me into the bushes.

Our father's shadow is on the grass. Then we see him, with no shirt on, wearing his sun-shield hat and his black scapula and his work pants tied at his waist with a piece of rope. In his left hand is a scythe which he swings back and forth not touching the grass, pale brown where the sun has baked it.

"What's he doing?"

My sister doesn't answer. Mitelin comes out from under the forsythia bush and streaks up the lawn. Our father lifts the scythe and she stops and heads back down the hill. Once I went under the forsythia bush and lay down in her spot, which is a smooth dip the size of her body. It was cool and dark and smelled of fur and flowers and dirt.

Our father walks down the hill, holding the scythe high above the grass. When he gets to the ditch, he walks along the edge to the end of our yard and then he crosses over and walks the length back up.

"What's he doing?" I ask again.

My sister pinches me hard on the arm, which means shut up. Now our father is standing in front of the ditch, looking up at the house with the handle of the scythe lifted onto his shoulder. Our mother says our father has a bomb in his head that keeps going off. He has been taken to the hospital a few times but he keeps coming back.

"Don't move," says my sister.

"Let's run," I say.

"Stupid, he'll see us."

My heart is beating fast, like Lily's when I hold her too tight.

"I know," says my sister. "Let's fly away."

"How can we?"

"We're birds. Remember? I'm a cardinal and you're a bluebird."

"I am a bluebird," I say.

"So," says my sister. "Bluebirds first."

"I don't want to go first."

"You have to."

"No."

"Then we aren't birds and we just have to sit here," says my sister.

We look out through the branches at our father, who is down in the ditch working the scythe in the tall grass. His chest is glistening with sweat. He swings the blade out and across the top of the grass sending green sprays up into the air.

After a while, my sister says she is bored and sneaks out of the bushes. I stay where I am, watching my father. I want to see it if his head blows up.

4

Finders Keepers

My sister is standing at the bottom of the driveway in her cowgirl outfit, trying to spin our father's rope belt like a lasso. The rope won't spin and she flings it into the bumblebee bushes. Even though I am afraid of the bees buzzing around the small white flowers, I run into the bushes to get the rope. As soon as I find it, my sister is on top of me, pulling the rope out of my hands. I pull back, hard, until my fingers start to turn purple. A bumblebee flies into the bushes near our faces, so close we can see the hairs vibrating on its black-and-yellow body.

My sister waits until the bee has flown away and then pushes me over onto the ground, pressing all her weight on top of me.

"It's mine," I say, holding on to the rope. "Finders keepers."

She jams her elbow into my neck. When I can hardly

breathe, I let go. She gets up and breaks from the bushes. I find the spot on my neck where she elbowed me, another place where I might get cancer. It already feels hot there.

I climb out of the bushes. My sister is at the bottom of the driveway, jumping in and out of the rope, which she has looped into a circle on the ground. I walk down to where she's jumping and watch. When she gets tired, I ask her if I can try. She says only for a minute.

While I'm jumping, she walks down to the ditch where the drainpipe comes in. She stands with her hands on her hips and stares at the ditch that runs the length of our front yard. Everything ends up there—dead leaves and twigs, old newspapers, Mitelin's chew bones, socks from the clothesline, the plastic missiles our neighbor Frankie Blackmore plays with, run-over birds and mice, things we've never seen before. Our father burns everything off. He lights a match and flames jump along the ditch, sending everything up into the air as fire or smoke, some of it floating up even higher as ash, so light it falls back down and blows around in tight circles along the scorched black bottom of the ditch.

While my sister is down there, I grab the rope and run up the driveway into the backyard. By the time I get to the mulberry tree she is on me, punching her fists into my back to get the rope away. Nothing she can do will make me let go this time.

But then she pushes my face into the ground and I can't breathe. I let go. She takes the rope and lets go of my head.

"You almost killed me."

"Good," she says, swinging the rope over her head. "Maybe next time you'll die."

"You'll die first," I say. "You're older."

In a second she is on me again, hitting me in the chest and neck with the rope. I try to grab it away but she keeps snapping it back.

"Okay," I say after she won't stop. "I'll die first."

She coils the rope in a loop around her elbow and thumb, then stands up and walks toward the house, smacking the rope on the pavement. I get up and walk in the opposite direction, down to the ditch. There might be something new in it.

First I look for anything shiny that's not tinfoil or glass. A few things sparkle but I already know what they are—a piece of smoky quartz, a metal band from one of our father's rakes, a crumpled piece of cellophane. Along the sides the ditch is singed black where the newest fires have been set. Sometimes the grass grows back but mostly it stays brown-black, the same color as the hair starting to cover my sister's V.

While I am down in the ditch, my sister comes around the side of the house, whipping the bushes with the rope belt. I lie flat in the ditch but right away she yells that she can see me. I stay facedown, not moving, even when I hear her start to come down the hill. Every time I breathe, tiny pieces of ash fly into my mouth and nose. The ash tastes like smoke and salt.

Now my sister is standing over me but I still don't move. Then I feel the sting of the rope on my back, through my play shirt. She does it again and this time I open my eyes a little. All I can see is black ash and grass.

"Are you dead yet?" my sister says. I can hear the rope spinning in the air above her head.

I don't answer. She keeps spinning the rope, waiting for me to move. Then she flings the rope onto my back. As fast as I can, I grab the rope and pull it under me. I brace myself because I know my sister is going to jump on me. But instead of jumping on me she says, "Jupiter is under you."

"No he isn't," I say.

I feel the rope under my belly.

"Jupiter's in the sky," I say.

"He'll jump out of the ground at you," my sister says.

I jump up, stuffing the rope under my shirt, and run for the driveway.

"You can have it," my sister yells after me.

I stop running and turn around and look at her. She's walking back up the hill in the front yard, toward the mimosa tree. I run after her.

"Why don't you want it?" I ask when I catch up with her.

"Because," she says.

She is climbing up into the mimosa tree.

"Then it's mine," I say.

"For now."

"Forever," I say.

"Until I say so," she says. She has reached the first notch of the tree and is climbing higher.

"When will that be?" I ask.

She doesn't answer. She has climbed as far as she can go and is turning around to sit on the last branch strong enough to hold her. I stand under the tree, the rope coiled like a snake under my shirt to keep my sister from getting it back. She is good at finding things, like Lily's tail when it fell off in the blackberry bushes, and our father's gun in the garage.

I look up at her but she's far away, high up in the branches staring way out past our yard. I pull the rope from under my shirt and wind it onto my arm. To test her I ask if she wants the rope back now. She just keeps looking past the branches of the tree.

The next day, when the cars are gone and my sister is at her tap class, I drag the can of gasoline from the garage down to the ditch. I take the rope from its hiding place and walk along to the end of the ditch past the forsythia bushes, and throw the rope in. I pour gasoline over it and then take a match out of the box I have stolen from the kitchen and light the rope. The fire catches and I step back, watching the flames jump along the rope until all of it is on fire, spilling black smoke. The rope twists back on itself like a fiery snake.

After the rope has burned ash white, I walk down into the ditch and stomp around on it. The ashes fly up and the wind carries them up farther along the ditch, which is black everywhere from the fires. I light a match and watch it burn down to where it almost touches my fingers. It's a game my sister taught me. The one who can hold on to the match the longest without letting go gets to keep the pack. My sister has a whole collection.

Now I take out another match and let it burn down. Even when the pain comes, I hold on.

g u r d e n

Up in the garden, we help our father dig out yellow onions. We are wearing our Chinese coolie hats and the striped sunsuits our neighbor Mrs. Campbell made. My sunsuit is too small for me. Every time I move it rips.

We watch our father lift the shovel and drive it into the dirt. He puts his workboot with no shoelaces on top of the shovel and pushes it deeper into the ground that is the color of baked clay. When the yellow onions come tumbling out of the dug-up dirt, we kneel down and grab them as fast as we can without getting in the way of the shovel while our father turns and turns the earth.

My sister always goes after the smaller onions because they roll the farthest away. Once, I went for an onion just as my father's shovel was coming down. Instead of digging in, he swung the shovel around and hit me with it. My sister heard my sunsuit tear when I stood up and turned away to keep from laughing. I don't have anything that you can see, not like my sister, who is getting dark there.

After the yellow onions have been dug up, we put them into the wheelbarrow our father keeps in the garage next to the broken player piano. It takes us a long time to get the wheelbarrow down the hill and to the basement window at the back of the house, where our father is waiting inside for us. All you can see is the top of his sun-shield hat and his bare sunburned shoulders and bare sunburned arms reaching up to grab the handfuls of onions we pass to him through the window.

When all the yellow onions have gone in through the basement window, my sister and I wait for our father to go somewhere in his car and then we sit in the shade in the front yard where it is cool and dark. Our faces and hands and fingernails are lined with dirt and the fronts of our legs are stained from kneeling in the red clay.

"You're too big for your sunsuit," says my sister. "When you stand up, I can see underneath."

"That's nothing," I say. "I've seen you where it's dark," I tell her.

We watch the shadows come out from under the bushes that are turning inky green. So many things could be hiding in them. Once my sister stuck her hand in a bush and when she pulled it out a spider was crawling on it. She let the spider go all the way up her arm past her elbow and then she flicked it upside down into the air.

"I don't want it to get dark yet," I say.

"It will," says my sister, and she stands and lifts the front of her sunsuit until her V is almost showing.

"I don't mean that," I tell her.

"Yes you do," she says, smoothing down her sunsuit. Then she calls Mitelin up from the ditch.

5

Bodies with Wings

Today Ed Riley is coming to mow the lawn. He comes every other Sunday in the summer to pay our father back for getting him a job with the government sorting mail. Our father doesn't work for the government anymore. He works at the American Legion hall. When we have to go with him and wait in the car, we count the Christmas lights strung partway along the roof that are never taken down. Sometimes an animal will move in the woods beyond the parking lot. Once, a man walked up to the car and looked in at us.

Usually it is dark by the time our father comes out of the building. We ride the back roads home without talking, everything lying low and black in the fields. The roads also are black except where lights flood the one-lane bridge near the turnoff to our house. Waiting to cross the bridge, I look up at the moths flying in and out of the bright yellow light.

Last night on the way home from the American Legion, my sister asked why our mother was in bed. Our father told us she had the flu but later, my sister told me it was because she lost a baby. It didn't show, not like with Mitelin when we could see the puppies moving around like fists inside her belly.

In the dark in the backseat, I pictured our mother in a long white nightgown that was swirling around her. In her arms was a baby. The baby slipped and fell down inside the folds of her gown and the gown kept swirling around until our mother also disappeared down inside the folds that rolled over her like giant white waves.

Waiting on the screened-in porch for Ed Riley, my sister and I read the funny papers. She is figuring out the Word Scramble. I never do. I cut out the paper dolls at the bottom of the page and make them clothes which I keep in a heart-shaped box. Sometimes I don't put any clothes on the paper dolls and even when they beg me to, I make them stay naked.

Whenever Ed Riley comes, my sister plays tricks on him. She'll get him to say funny-sounding words like goil for girl and arful for awful. He's from New York. Our mother said he was raised in an orphanage, but he told us he spends every Christmas with his mother in the house where he grew up.

When Ed Riley gets to our house, he is already sweating. That's because he doesn't have a car and has to walk or take the bus. Our father meets him by the garage, where he is pouring gasoline into the lawn mower. He is wearing his hat and his back is covered with sun blisters from working in the garden.

Ed Riley stands watching, his red hair shaved in a crew cut like our neighbor Frankie Blackmore's in the summer. His face and arms are covered with freckles. So are his legs. His zories are yellow. Our father's zories are black.

After he wheels the lawn mower down to the driveway, my father tells me to get Ed Riley a clean rag from the basement. I don't want to go. One of the neighborhood cats is down there. She fell in through the open basement window and broke her leg. Now she won't let anyone near her.

"You go," I whisper to my sister on the porch.

"Scaredy," she says.

At the top of the basement stairs, my sister puts on the light. We walk about halfway down before we see the cat, lying in the corner near the water heater. The leg that is broken sticks out straight from her body, like Lily's when she licks herself. The floor around her is covered with clumps of blue dust. She bares her teeth at us but no sound comes out.

"I'll wait here," I tell my sister.

I sit down on the steps while my sister goes into the laundry room. The cat watches me with her milky eyes. She is the mother of two kittens who ran away and another one who ate poison and died. We buried the poisoned one in the backyard behind the woodpile. We didn't tell our father because he would have taken her. He thinks she ran away.

My sister comes out with the rag, a piece of the nightgown I was wearing when she pushed me into the living-room fan. The fan is the stand-up one that we sometimes sing into when our mother and father aren't home. When I fell into it, the fan sucked up the hem of my nightgown and shredded it before my sister yanked the plug out.

We climb back up the stairs. At the top, I hear Ed Riley's voice. Sometimes, in the middle of talking, he'll stutter. When this happens, he cries out in a way that sounds like an animal. My mother says he has a speech impediment. My sister says he is just stupid.

At the landing, my sister keeps going up the stairs to get ready for her tap class. I bring the rag out to Ed Riley.

"Hiya, g-g-goilie," he says in his thick, slow voice, as

he picks me up and twirls me around. It hurts where his thumbs are pressing into my underarms. I let go of the rag and it falls away into the grass.

After Ed Riley puts me down, I find the rag on the ground and bring it to him. When he takes it, a whimpering noise comes out of his mouth. My mother says it's part of his speech problem but my sister says it's because Ed Riley is more of an animal than a human.

Our father wheels the lawn mower into the front yard and Ed Riley goes into the garage to put the gas can away. I run to the back of the garage and move the broken slat to one side to look in at him, but it's too dark to see. Even though I'm afraid of Ed Riley, I feel sorry for him. He wants us to think he has a mother. My sister says he did have a mother and that she was a laughing hyena.

Ed Riley is mowing around the apple tree. He never clears the apples from the ground first, so they come flying out of the machine in big chunks. Once, Mitelin got hit in the face by one and her eye closed up.

My sister comes out of the house wearing her black leotard and over that her red-and-gold spangled tap vest and skirt. Her hair is braided and twisted into a loop around the top of her head and she is carrying her black patent-leather tap-shoe case.

Our father has gone somewhere in his car.

"What about the mother cat?" I ask my sister. We have to move her before our father finds her.

"Wait till I get back," she says.

I walk with her to the bottom of the driveway. Lily runs from under the forsythia down into the drainpipe. I watch my sister walk up the street until all I can see is the light jumping around like little stars on her vest and skirt.

Before I get to the top of the driveway, the lawn mower cuts off. I run into the bushes so Ed Riley won't see me when he wheels the mower into the garage.

After he goes in, I run to the back of the garage and move the slat. At first all I can see is shadows. Then I see Ed Riley sitting on a wooden crate near the player piano. He pulls the nightgown rag out of his pocket and wipes his head.

"I see you, g-g-goilie," he says. I hold my breath and keep my eye wide open.

"I see you," he says again.

I let out my breath.

"Do you really have a mother?" I ask.

He doesn't answer.

"Do you?" I ask again.

"My mother is p-p-p-pretty," he says. "Like, like, like, like." Then he is stuttering so violently that his head juts forward into the light of the open door. His mouth draws into a tight circle and he lets out that noise. When he can speak again, he says, "L-l-like your mother."

All of a sudden I want to run to my mother, but I'm afraid my father will come home and find me with her. Instead, I run to the woodpile where we buried the kitten who ate poison. With a stick I start digging up the dirt. Then I use my hands, and when I see the top of the shoe box, I stop digging and lift it out.

In the basement, the mother cat is still lying in the corner by the water heater. Her fur looks blue in the dirty light. I put the box down near her and step back.

She doesn't move, so I push the box closer to her, turning my face away from the smell. She keeps watching me and then her head starts shaking and white foam comes out of her mouth. Her eyes roll up inside her head. I run up the stairs to tell Ed Riley what is happening to the mother cat.

When he sees her in the basement lying on her side, he lets out that noise. Blood has come out of her nose and mouth.

"Don't tell your f-f-f-father," he says to me and then he picks up the dead mother cat and holds her.

"Don't t-t-t-tell," he says again.

Then I say, "Don't you tell your mother." His mouth opens and no sound comes out.

"You don't have a mother," I say.

His head jerks and his spit is flying out.

"I don't either," I say, but Ed Riley shakes his head at me.

"Y-y-your m-m-mother's p-p-pretty," he says.

Outside, he wraps the dead mother cat in the lawn-mower rag and fits her into the shoebox on top of the kitten. He doesn't turn his face away from the smell.

Even though it's one of our secret places, I take Ed Riley up to the woodpile. We put the box back in the hole and cover it with dirt. Then we stamp on the ground until it is flat again and throw some leaves on top.

"Don't tell," Ed Riley says and then walks down the hill to the bottom of the driveway, where he'll wait for our father to take him to the bus stop in town.

Later, when my sister comes back from tap class, I tell her what happened. We go up and look at the grave. My sister makes a cross out of two sticks and then braids them with dandelions and three-leaf clovers. I don't say anything about Ed Riley or his mother.

At the bottom of the driveway, my sister shows me the new steps she learned in class today. Sometimes when she dances, her arms fly out and go in circles over her head. But now she just holds on to her waist, her elbows jutting out at sharp angles to her ribs. Her feet are moving very fast, their shadows lifting off the ground and then coming back down, light, dark, light, dark, light.

"Here's the new part," she says. She twirls around and goes down on one knee. Then she jumps back and her arms fly out while she taps in place. The spangles on her vest and skirt shimmy and shake. One of them drops off but she doesn't notice. It disappears in the wind.

For an instant I look away because I see our mother standing at the top of the driveway.

"Watch!" my sister yells to me, and she taps backwards holding her arms out straight in front of her, making wide circles with her palms. She goes up on her toes, holding her knees. When she lets go, she taps forward really fast, keeping her hands on her hips.

"Here's the best part," she says. Her arms go up over her head in a circle and she rocks on her heels. Then her legs fly apart and she does the splits. While she is holding the splits, I look up at the top of the driveway. Our mother isn't there.

Even later, we sit in the dark on the screened-in porch watching for lightning bugs. They blink in the bushes and the trees. Some of them just hang in the air. After a while, the headlights of our father's car shine into the driveway. Dozens of bodies with wings swim in the light. The bodies fly and float in the current and then the light goes through them and they are gone.

milky way

At the grocery store, my mother gets into Mr. Johnston's checkout line. In our cart are hot dogs, hot dog buns, mustard, catsup, frozen peas and carrots, soy sauce, peanut butter, root beer, milk, and vanilla wafers. My mother is wearing her hair in a French twist and her earrings are black pearls that match the buttons going down the front of her dress. She is working at the studio again but she isn't making costumes like she used to. She sits at a desk.

When the line moves up, I help her take the groceries out of the cart and put them on the counter. Mr. Johnston watches her and when she looks up, he smiles. Then he signals to me to get a candy bar from the rack. I take a Milky Way bar.

Mr. Johnston watches my mother write the check for

the groceries. His eyes go from the top of her ginger-colored hair down to her eyes and lips and then to her neck.

While he's watching, I wonder what it would be like if Mr. Johnston was my father. He wears a red bow tie and his hairline starts way back from his forehead, which is always shiny. On his pinky finger is a gold ring with a flat black stone. Sometimes he kids my mother about taking dance lessons from her because he knows she used to be a dancer, but tonight he just loads the bags into the cart and puts the check under his register drawer. Before we leave, my mother reminds me to thank him for the candy bar. He tells me to take good care of my mother, to help her with the groceries when we get home. While he is talking, my mother puts a thumb and a finger up to her black pearl earring and rubs it.

I say good night to Mr. Johnston.

"Night, Bill," says my mother.

On the way home, the bags of groceries rustle and squeak in the backseat. I sit up front next to my mother, watching her face in the dark while she drives. I want to ask her what her secrets are, to know them like I know my own. Before I say anything we are back home.

In the driveway, the light from the top of the porch shines into the front seat. My mother looks beautiful, her face full of shadows.

I want to say that I love her, even more than Mr. Johnston does, but I don't.

She tells me to go inside, she is going to sit awhile longer in the car. I want to stay with her, where my sister and not even my father can find me. Instead I open the car door on my side and step onto the driveway. The black pavement twinkles with bits of ground-up glass.

From the porch steps, I turn back around. My mother is staring at me through the windshield.

6

Mr. Romeo

Frankie Blackmore is hiding in the bushes. He thinks I am inside counting to one hundred, but I'm outside waiting for him on the front steps. As he comes around the side of the house, the tops of the bushes part and sway. I move onto the porch so he can't see me unless he looks straight up. He keeps cutting through the bushes. First I see the top of his head, which is flat because of his summer crew cut. Then I see his hands moving down. He puts one hand behind him and leans against the bricks. Then he moves the other hand down inside his pants. I watch his face. His eyes are half closed and his mouth is a little bit open. He keeps holding himself, moving his hand around and around. He shuts his eyes. With both hands he squeezes, faster and faster until he is rising up on his toes, his head tipped back against the bricks. Then his hands stop and he lets out a cry like he is being hurt.

It is the first time I have seen Frankie do this. My sister says she has seen him do it a lot. I watch his hands to see where they will go but his hands stay still. His face looks like one of the saints on the holy cards in my prayer book. When he looks like Frankie Blackmore again, I kneel down and press my face against the porch railing.

"Frankie," I say. "You're dead."

His face is the same color as the bricks.

"Go find your stupid sister," he says. He grabs onto the railing and pulls himself up onto the porch.

According to the rules, Frankie has to stay where he is until I bring my sister in or she makes it back. Usually, when we play Dead Man's Tag, I can't find Frankie. He's a good hider.

I leave Frankie on the porch and go around to the backyard to hunt for my sister. Suddenly, she breaks from behind the apple tree and races past me down the hill. I run after her but she's too quick. By the time I get to the front porch, she and Frankie are jumping down behind the bushes.

"You can't go in there," I call to my sister from the railing.

"She can if she wants to," Frankie answers.

"There are ticks," I say.

"Who's afraid of ticks?" Frankie wants to know.

Once a tick bit the back of my sister's neck. By the time she found it, the tick was as big as the mole on Mitelin's cheek. My sister flushed the tick down the toilet, its fat gray body going around and around.

"We're afraid of ticks," I tell Frankie.

"You're afraid of ticks," Frankie says. He and my sister head deeper into the bushes. I climb the railing to make the jump, but then I stop. The tops of the bushes shake and sway. I try to picture what Frankie and my sister are doing in there. All I can see is a tick growing big as my father's fist.

After dinner, in our room, I tell my sister what Frankie was doing in the bushes.

"Show me," she says.

I climb across her bed and stand with my back to the wall. I put one hand behind me and the other one on my V.

"He moved his hand around and around," I tell her.

"So show me," she says.

"Like this." I do it a little bit. My V tingles.

"Is that all?" she says.

"He went up on his toes with his eyes closed and he cried out."

My sister is smiling.

"You should see what he really does," she says, "with no pants on."

I want to ask her what Frankie does with no pants on. Instead I look around her side of the room—at the poodle drawings over her desk and her baton lying on the windowsill, her holy-water angel near the door and her blue and white pom-poms hanging from the doorknob I am not allowed to touch. I can feel her eyes on me, waiting for me to ask.

"What does Frankie do?"

"Lots of things."

"Like what."

"You'll see," she says. Then she tells me to leave because she wants to play her Beatles and Chubby Checker records. On my way out, I dip my finger into the holy water and make the sign of the cross.

"It means you're a sinner," she says.

"I am not."

"With Frankie you will be," she says. Then she puts on a Beatles record.

"I like George."

"Too ugly," she says. "I like Paul."

Later, with the door closed, I put on my Chopin record and lie down. On the album cover, Chopin is sitting at the piano in a black velvet suit with tails that hang over the back of the piano bench. He is wearing black velvet slippers and one foot is resting on the middle pedal. His hands are long and pale. So is his face. I bring the album cover to my lips and kiss Chopin on the mouth. I shut my eyes but instead of Chopin's hands, I see Frankie's in the bushes. I want to hear the music. All I hear is Frankie making that noise like he is being tortured.

"Frankie!" I cry.

My sister comes in without knocking.

"You were calling for Frankie," she says. "I'm telling."

"Don't," I say, but I know she will. Then I tell her to get out, because she didn't knock. It's one of our rules.

After she leaves, I listen to the rest of Chopin. When the music stops, the room is so dark that I can't see. I find the album cover on the bed and bring it to my face. Without being able to see his hands at the piano or the outline of his pale white face, I say to Chopin, whose music is still in me, "You're mine."

I'm hiding in the front yard behind the forsythia bushes. Through the branches, I can see Mitelin rooting in the ditch. She is wearing a piece of an old bed sheet because she is in heat. We found drops on the dining-room floor and told our mother. My sister said it means Mitelin could have puppies if Aloysius climbs on her. We're supposed to take turns watching to make sure the sheet doesn't come off.

I'm hiding from Frankie. He's not a fast runner like my sister but he has good eyes. Once, when we were playing Dead Man's Tag inside, he found my sister in the closet in the basement without looking anywhere else first. I was hiding in the corner behind the water heater and he came down the stairs and went into the closet, in the dark with her, and closed the door. Instead of running to the safety zone, I went over to the closet and listened. When I heard their breathing, I ran.

Now I can see Frankie through the bushes. I make a run for the safety zone but trip over the stump of the black oak tree and land hard on the ground. Before I can get up, Frankie is there.

"You're dead," he says, standing over me.

"I fell."

"Because you're a girl," says Frankie.

"So."

"So, you're dead."

"Did you kill my sister?" I ask him.

"Not yet," he says. "But I will."

I stand up and we race down the hill. By the time we get to the mimosa tree, my legs are burning. Frankie is ahead of me, his body hard with speed. My legs won't go any faster.

"Stop!" I yell, but Frankie keeps running and disappears across the top of the yard. I slow down and start watching the bushes because I know he's in there. Near the blue hydrangea, his blond crew cut flashes against the bricks.

"I see you," I tell him.

"I see you," he says.

The flowers on the blue hydrangea quiver and shake. A bumblebee lands on one and clasps a tiny blue petal between its legs.

"What are you doing?" I ask Frankie.

"What do you think?" he says.

"Counting?"

"See for yourself."

I push back the branches of the blue hydrangea and step in. Frankie's pants are down around his ankles and he is holding himself. He squeezes and his penis starts to grow. He keeps squeezing and two red lipstick dots like eyes appear at the tip and then a red line that curves into a smile. Frankie is smiling too.

"It's Mr. Romeo," he says. "Do you want to kiss him?"

"No."

"Why not?"

"He's ugly."

Frankie keeps squeezing.

"Stop it," I say, but I keep looking.

"Come on," Frankie says. But Frankie's penis is shrinking back inside his hands.

"Mr. Romeo's gone," I say.

"No," says Frankie. "He's hiding." Frankie reaches down and pulls up his pants.

"Does my sister know him?" I ask.

"Sure."

"Did she kiss him?"

"Why don't you ask her."

Frankie flips back the branches of the blue hydrangea and runs to look for my sister. I slide down the bricks and sit. I don't care if a tick gets on me. I even want one to. When I turn my head, something on the ground shimmers. It's Frankie's lipstick. I reach for it and hold it up to the light. On the bottom, the label says "Rendez-vous Red." I twist off the cap and roll the tube all the way up. Without letting it touch, I hold the lipstick to my nose to see if it smells like Frankie. It might be Frankie. Then I twist the tube back down and put the lipstick in my pocket.

After Frankie goes home, my sister and I lie in the shade in the front yard, away from the smell of the sump pump, which is overflowing. Mitelin makes her way up from the ditch. The tied-on sheet is stained with dark spots. She lies down on the grass between us and stretches out. I move over so that I am lying back to back with her. My sister rests her head on Mitelin's belly.

"I saw Mr. Romeo today," I tell my sister.

"Now you know," she says.

"Did you kiss him?" I ask, sitting up.

"Did you?"

My sister rolls away from Mitelin and me. In the deep shade, her hair looks ginger-colored, like our mother's.

"What was it like?" I ask her.

She turns around to face us and the sun reflecting off the windows of the house makes her frown. She starts to stretch her leg out toward Mitelin but stops.

"Watch out for the blood," she tells me.

I move away from Mitelin, but I can still feel her warm body behind me. Her smell is strong, like wet leaves. We stay in the shade until my sister says it's time to change Mitelin's sheet, and then we lead her up the stairs into the house.

In our room, I show my sister the lipstick.

"Put some on," she says.

"I don't want to."

"I will," she says. She takes the lipstick from me and puts it on in front of the mirror over her dresser. She presses her lips together like our mother does to make the color spread evenly.

"Your turn," she tells me when she's done.

I knock the lipstick out of her hand onto the bed.

"What a baby," she says. Then she smiles at me with her big red mouth and some of the color comes off on her teeth.

"Frankie's in you now," I tell her.

"You're cracked," she says, but she walks over to the mirror and opens her mouth wide and sticks out her tongue, moving it up and down like she's checking.

"See?" I say. Then, to show her I'm not afraid, I put my finger in her holy-water angel on my way out of the room, and dab some on my wrist like perfume.

"That's nothing," says my sister. "You're still a baby."

In the dark, I listen to Chopin. Even though I am lying still on my bed, everything inside of me is moving. My mother said that Chopin was very young when he died, and that he was a romantic. No one knows I have given my heart to him, not even my sister.

p y r a m i d s

Our father has on a suit and tie and our mother is wearing her emerald-green cocktail dress. She is carrying a small green purse and her pretend-mink stole, because the movie theater they are going to is air-conditioned.

We watch from our bedroom window as they come out of the house. My sister says the movie they are going to see is about the Egyptians and most of them get killed.

We watch our mother and father get into the car. Through the windshield, she looks pretty and he looks handsome. Her earrings sparkle when she leans forward to put her purse in the glove compartment.

"Do you think they're in love?" I ask my sister.

"No," she says.

After the car backs down the driveway, my sister and I stay at the window. I think about the Egyptians. Most of them were slaves, and the people who whipped them were also slaves.

After a while my sister and I drift away from the window. She goes into our parents' room to look around. I follow her as far as their bedroom door and watch as she looks on top of our mother's and father's dressers and on the night tables next to their bed. On our father's side of the room is a wooden card table covered with brown file boxes tied with string. On our mother's side is a vanity. In the middle, on top, is a mirrored tray crowded with perfumes, lipsticks, a box of Kleenex, and a powder box with a blue puff inside it.

"What are you looking for?" I ask my sister.

"Stuff," she says.

"What stuff?"

"Anything."

I go back to our room and lie down on my bed. I picture my parents at the movies, my mother sitting in her mink stole and my father next to her in his good suit and tie. On the screen the Egyptians are being tortured and killed. I try to imagine what it is the Egyptians lived for, but nothing comes to mind. Then I remember the pyramids, how they were built by thousands and thousands of slaves and how hundreds of them got sealed up inside the tombs or fell to their deaths from the tops of the pyramids.

I wonder how the movie will end, if anyone will be saved. Then I listen for my sister in our parents' bedroom. She is moving around, opening their drawers and closets, looking at all their things.

I close my eyes and when it feels like I am falling from the top of a giant tomb, I open my eyes again. I get out of bed and go into my parents' bedroom. My sister tells me to get out but I keep opening my parents' closets and drawers, looking under their bed, in their boxes and bags, on top of their dressers, wherever there might be something.

Summer
1965

7

Blizzard

My sister reaches for the windshield-wiper knob because on our pretend-trip it has started to snow. She pretend—puts on the headlights. Then she tells me she is slowing to forty-five because it is getting too hard to see.

"We might have to pull over," she says.

She is concentrating, which she is good at, leaning forward with both hands on the wheel. Mitelin is asleep in the backseat. Her paws are twitching, which means she's dreaming. I tell my sister to hurry and look at Mitelin before it's too late. She tells me to shut up and let her drive or the car might slide off the road and flip over. I picture the car leaving the road, flying up and then upside down over the white trees, my sister and Mitelin and me floating around inside like astronauts in a space capsule.

"We better stop for a while," says my sister. "I can't see."

She turns the wheel while looking in the rearview mirror and pretend—pulls over. We are in the burned-up car parked on cinder blocks beside the driveway. The tires and rims are lying out on the grass. Sometimes our father sleeps in this car. We'll pass by him on our way down the driveway, his arms thrown up over his head and his shoes with the taps on the bottom sticking out the punched-out window.

"We could have crashed," says my sister after she has pretend—turned off the engine. She points to the tires and the rims. "Look at all those wrecks."

Mitelin moans in her sleep. The sun has come up over the top of the garage and is shining down into the front seat. It is boiling hot, but my sister says we have to keep the windows rolled up so the snow doesn't blow in. Out my window, I pretend the snow is flying by, that it is drifting high up against the bushes and the house and the trees, that it is almost up to the windows of the car.

"Where are we going?" I ask my sister.

Her arms are crossed and she is staring straight ahead through the space between the dashboard and the steering wheel.

"Away," she says.

"Where?"

"I'll think of a place."

We sit, pretend-watching the snow. In the backseat, in her dream, Mitelin is trying to bark but it sounds like someone is squeezing shut her muzzle. We tried to get Lily into the car by holding out carrots to her but she wouldn't come. Lily is wild but she is still ours.

I didn't bring anything with me on the pretend-trip except for a can of root beer and the black bra with no straps I found a long time ago in the ditch. When my sister saw the bra, she said I shouldn't worry about growing any breasts while we're on our trip. Hers are already growing but every time I ask, she won't let me see them. She brought her Chubby Checker records and her pompoms. For Mitelin we filled her water bowl and picked up all the chew bones we could find around the yard.

"We might have to sit a long time," my sister says after we already have been sitting a long time. Mitelin is awake now, trying to drink from her water bowl on the floor in the backseat. First she tries to get down on the floor, but there isn't enough room. Then she sits with her back legs on the seat and her front legs hanging over, but she can't get her head down far enough to reach the bowl. Finally, I climb into the backseat and put her bowl where she can reach it. She drinks the water with her long, flat, pink tongue and then she keeps licking the inside of the bowl until it is dry.

"I think it's a blizzard by now," says my sister. The back of her head is round. Mitelin's is square.

"What if Dad sees us?" I say.

"He can't in all this snow," says my sister. Then she tells me, "If he comes out, get down on the floor."

"But he'll see Mitelin."

"Pull her down with you!" my sister yells. Then she's crying, which she almost never does. She presses her fists to her eyes to stop the tears. Today our father came after her with the rope belt. He caught her at the bottom of the stairs, trying to run away, and chased her all the way up to our bedroom. Now she has red-and-white stripes on the backs of her legs.

"Do you want me to drive?" I ask.

"I want you to shut up," she says.

"Okay," I say. She is still crying.

Once we were in a real blizzard, riding over the mountains with our mother to visit our father in the hospital. All night we stayed in the car by the side of the road while the snow and the wind whipped around us and the car shuddered and rocked. When the snow blew up into the air, we saw the headlights of the other cars parked along the road shining into the storm. We listened to the radio and ate some of the cake decorated like an American flag our mother had bought for our father. We had to let Mitelin out of the car, and when she got back inside, she licked the snow off the seat that had gusted in.

After that we fell asleep. The next day, the sun came out and we could see the snow clinging to the heavy branches of the fir trees and hear it squeaking and hissing under the wheels of the car as we drove back onto the road. For as far as we could see and in every direction the whole world was white.

At the hospital, we forgot the cake in the car and Mitelin ate the rest of it, even the box. Our father wouldn't see us, so we came back out and drove home through the snow that dropped from the branches of the giant trees onto the wet black road.

Now I try to picture the snow being blown sideways in the wind. Instead there are the bumblebee bushes and the sidewalk to the porch that is covered with smashed mulberries and the hole in the screen door stuffed with a sock. I smooth the fur on Mitelin's leg and put my hand in between the top of her haunch and her ribs. It is my favorite part of her except for the bump at the top of her head.

After we have been silent again for a while, I ask my sister if we are still in a blizzard.

First she says yes and then she says, "This is a stupid idea."

"Why?"

"Because there isn't any blizzard and we're not going anyplace."

"Yes we are."

"Where?"

I try to think of someplace.

"See," she says. "It's stupid."

"Where do you want to go?" I ask.

"Anyplace!" she says, hitting the steering wheel with her fists.

After that, we don't talk for a while. I stay in the backseat with Mitelin, who is sleeping with her head in my lap. When it gets too hot, I lift Mitelin off me and climb into the front where there is shade.

"You don't have to stare," my sister says even though I only looked at her for a second.

Out the front window on the hood of the car is a dragonfly with blue-green wings that have lacy, see-through veins. The heat lifts off the car in waves around him, shimmying into the bright air. It could be a blizzard, the way everything is white with light.

"Come on," I tell my sister. "We still have a long way to go."

She looks at me, frowning, and then she sighs and puts her hands on the wheel and pretend–starts up the car. She pretend-pulls onto the highway, and I remind her to put on the high beams because the snow is blowing and drifting across the road.

"Are we going back?" I say after she has been pretend-driving for a while.

"Never," she says.

I look straight ahead. There's no traffic except for our car, with our two round heads and Mitelin's square one. We keep traveling through the storm, away from our house to a place we don't know the name of yet where the snow is getting deeper and deeper.

c r e p e   m y r t l e

This time my sister really is running away. She says I can follow her once she makes it down the driveway but that if I get caught she'll punch me fifty times on the arm. I run upstairs to watch from our bedroom window. If she gets down the driveway, she can run across the street to the Elliots' house. Past their yard is a shortcut to the highway.

There's no screen on the window and I stick my head way out. She has the loaf of bread she snuck from the freezer and is past the century plants at the bottom of the driveway. Then, before she jumps the ditch, our father runs past the crepe myrtle and grabs her, twisting her arms up over her head. The loaf of bread rips open and chunks of it scatter onto the driveway and in the grass.

My sister bucks to get away but our father holds on, lifting her off the ground as he walks up the driveway. A bird flies down to get a chunk of bread, then another one. The driveway is filling up with birds fighting over the bread. Some fly away with the pieces, up into the trees and onto the telephone wires. My sister is still bucking and twisting but our father has her.

After that it's quiet. A bird calls to another bird. I walk over to the bedroom door and listen. Nothing. Then I hear my sister coming up the stairs.

8

Mustang

In the Vollmers' above-ground pool, sunlight shimmers and glints as my sister moves through the water. She has been in there for fifteen minutes, swimming around and around without touching the sides while I stand lookout on a chair next to the pool. I don't go in the Vollmers' pool. There are slugs on the bottom and the sides because the Vollmers don't have a filter. My sister says they don't need a filter. She says the slugs keep the bottom and the sides clean.

In the water, her black bathing suit is a shiny streak and her bathing cap is a white oval moving just ahead of it. Her pace is so steady that the waves make a pattern around the pool, lapping the sides. When I am not watching for the Vollmers' dogs, I squint hard into the water against the jumpy light.

After her swim, my sister sits on the ladder pulling

at her suit so it puffs with air. "Come on," I tell her. She just lets go of her suit to hear the smacking sound it makes against her ribs. She is starting to get breasts. At night, I dream about getting them, like the ones our neighbor Peggy Spencer has. When we sunbathe with her in the backyard in our bathing suits, you can see how big her breasts are when she bends over. She has a boyfriend she meets after school in the woods. He doesn't go to school. He works for a trucking company, washing the trucks. Peggy brags to us that she is seeing him even though her parents forbid her to. I know he touches her breasts when they are in the woods together. I would, to know how it will feel when I have them.

My sister climbs out of the pool and puts her clothes on over her wet bathing suit. I drag the chair back over to the patio and then we take the shortcut home through the blackberry bushes. We roll down our sleeves and pull our hair back with rubber bands so the brambles won't catch at us. There aren't many berries left, but we find enough to fill my sister's swim cap. We pass the cap back and forth, eating the berries and picking new ones. The berries leave inky stains inside the cap. When you first bite into them, they taste like pool water.

Lily still runs back here, where she lost her tail. We leave her the berries that are low on the bushes. She'll stand on her hind legs to eat the berries higher up. If she sees us she stays still but she never runs away from us. When she lifts her leg, we can see the bald patch of skin where her tail fell off. With her leg up high and straight, she'll bend her head to that spot and work it and work it with her tongue.

There is a shortcut to the shortcut which we take to get away from the brambles and out of the sun. Waves of heat are rippling the air. This shortcut goes through the woods where our neighbor Peggy Spencer meets her boyfriend. He is not too tall and has shiny black hair that he combs straight back. Peggy said she taught him dances like the mashed potatoes and the peppermint twist. Then my sister asked what he taught her and Peggy said the French kiss. Later, my sister told me it wasn't a dance. When I was in the bathroom, I stuck out my tongue in the mirror and kept looking at it until it didn't look like a tongue. It was more like an animal that was just connected to me in my mouth.

In the woods now it is cool and dark. There is a smell of mud and old leaves. I follow my sister along the path. Her blond ponytail hangs to the middle of her back. My ponytail is dark, the color of tree bark. It won't grow past the bottom of my neck.

"Let's pretend we're horses," I say.

"Not today."

She wants to act older. When we're horses, usually she's a palomino and I'm a mustang. We start out walking and then we build to a gallop being chased by men on horseback trying to catch us with ropes and tame us. We'll lose the men coming through the woods and then lie down winded at the edge of the field where it is shaded and hidden from the rise.

I'm pretending I'm a horse when my sister stops me and whispers the name of Peggy's boyfriend. He is up ahead, leaning against a tree that has no bark where all the initials are carved into it. My sister says she'll wait until she is going steady to carve hers. She makes it sound like it might be soon, but the only boys she knows are Frankie Blackmore and Duane Shields and she says they are turning into hoods.

"Don't talk," she says as we get closer to Peggy's boyfriend. From the back he already looks like a hood in his white T-shirt and jeans. Peggy told us he has a tattoo of a naked dancer above his left nipple. She says that when he squeezes his palms together, the dancer wiggles around.

All of a sudden, he turns around and pins us with his eyes. He doesn't look nice or mean, just alert.

"You're the girls Peggy used to watch," he says as we're about to go by him. My sister stops and I stop behind her.

"Are you waiting for her?" my sister asks. He looks her over, which makes me afraid for her.

"Maybe," he says. Then looking right at her, almost

glaring, he says, "You don't need a baby-sitter now that you're a big girl, do you?"

"No," she says. She slowly backs up, almost stepping on me.

"Well, you sure are a big girl," he says.

"She isn't," I say, and then I run as fast as I can toward the light flooding into the woods from the field. When I get to the rise, I turn around, but my sister isn't there. I walk back down toward the woods, which have a cool, damp smell like a cave. Where the path goes in there is sunlight in the shape of a sword and behind it a black road, black trees, black leaves. My sister walks out and puts her arm up over her eyes. I run to her.

"What happened?" I ask her.

"Nothing."

"Tell me."

"I said nothing."

"Are you going to tell Peggy?"

"Leave me alone," she says. She breaks away, running fast like when we play horses.

I try to keep up with her but she doesn't slow down until we are clear of the field, where our neighborhood begins. Her ponytail is practically all the way out of the rubber band.

"I'm a mustang!" I call out to her, but she doesn't stop or turn around.

She is way ahead of me, whipping the sidewalk with a

branch of forsythia she broke off as we were coming through the field.

In the Vollmers' pool my sister floats on her back, her arms and legs making star points in the bright blue water. Her eyes are closed and her hair floats free, spiraling out behind her head like a watery halo. She is wearing her new purple-and-black two-piece with the yellow bows that tie at her hips. Her stomach is flat but her chest hasn't gotten any bigger. I can tell she is worried she isn't going to grow much more because of the way she looked at herself in the hall mirror before we left the house, like she was mad at her body. At least she has hips. Mine are straight, like a boy's.

After she climbs out of the pool, we go home the long way. We haven't taken the shortcut since we saw Peggy's boyfriend that time in the woods. Today Peggy's coming to sunbathe with us and when we get home she is already out in the backyard. She sets up the sprinkler so we can run under it. We keep our zories on so we won't step on any bees.

My sister gets Peggy to run under the sprinkler with us. She has to duck way down for the spray. It is hard not to look at her top. While we're taking turns with the sprinkler, Peggy's boyfriend walks into the backyard. He isn't supposed to be here, but Peggy doesn't tell him to leave. She goes over to him while my sister and I stay by the sprinkler.

First he puts his hand on her shoulder and then it goes around her back and he pulls her toward him. Peggy turns around and tells us to go lie down on our beach towels, which are spread out in the shade in the side yard.

"They're going to make out," my sister says. She slaps at the water spray. Then she splashes some into my face.

"Quit it," I say.

"Quit what," she says, and splashes me again.

"I'll tell Peggy," I say.

"Why don't you tell her boyfriend instead," says my sister. She runs to her towel and throws herself down. I stay by the sprinkler, trying to watch, but Peggy turns around again and waves at me to go. I walk a few steps and then bend down like I'm fixing my zori. I turn and see them kissing. Peggy's bathing-suit strap is down on one side and his hands are moving across her back. He sees me and keeps looking at me while his fingers pinch and rub Peggy all over until it feels like my breasts are starting to grow. I put my head down. A bumblebee is climbing on a clover bud, holding on while the clover sways under his black weight. He lets go and flies up at me. I run to my towel so fast that my zories come off.

"I almost got stung," I tell my sister. She is lying facedown on her Paul McCartney beach towel.

"Are you okay?" I ask.

Bird & Bee images.

"Shut up," she says.

I sit down on my George Harrison beach towel. The sprinkler is still on, waving its plume of water back and forth across the lawn.

"I bet they're doing the French twist," I tell my sister.

"French kiss, stupid," she says. The sun is moving around the side of the house, cutting deep angles off the roof and off the backs of my sister's legs. I put my head down on my towel and lie still, feeling the sun. The only sound is the sprinkler going back and forth. A dragonfly lands on my sister's bathing suit, at the small of her back. Its blue wings are see-through and its head and body are the color of bottle glass. Even though he isn't moving, his body is pulsing, picking up light.

Probably Peggy and her boyfriend are kissing very hard. I kiss the back of my hand until it hurts. Like that. Then a shadow comes up over my shadow in the grass. I'm afraid it's him but when I turn around it's Peggy. Her lips aren't fiery red, but her eyes are puffy like she's been crying.

"Are you okay?" I ask her.

"We broke up," she says. My sister rolls over and sits up, so fast that I think she is going to do something violent. But she looks happy.

"How'd it happen?" she asks. Peggy tells me to move my legs over so she can sit next to me on the towel. She leans back on one arm and her breasts are practically touching my shoulder.

"He wanted me to marry him," she says. "But I told him I wasn't ready." Peggy is sixteen. We don't know how old her ex-boyfriend is, but he looks old enough to be a man.

My sister turns her head away, smiling. Peggy puts her hand up to her forehead and starts to cry. Every time she sobs, her big breasts brush against me. My sister cups her hands under her smaller ones, posing on her towel like she is a movie star.

I want to get up and run like a mustang, but I don't have my zories on and the yard is full of bees.

aloysius

From the bedroom window, my sister and I watch Aloysius climb on Mitelin. He holds on with his front legs while his back legs follow Mitelin around. She twists and turns, biting the air, but Aloysius holds on. He stays on top of her, rounding over her again and again.

They move from the apple tree to the fence that goes around the sump pump to the garage.

"Does it hurt her?" I ask my sister.

"Of course," she says. "It hurts him too."

We watch their bodies. Mitelin's neck arches across her back. The whites of her eyes shine. Aloysius stays tight behind her, and when he growls, a feeling goes through me like electricity. I put one hand down on my V, but I don't do anything.

"She might have puppies," I say.

"I know," says my sister. A shiny black fly lands on her hand and she smashes it.

When Aloysius finally climbs down, his penis is almost touching the ground. It hangs between his legs like a piece of hose. Mitelin runs under the bushes by the side of the house and Aloysius goes up and down along the fence until he finds an opening into his yard.

My sister and I run downstairs and out of the house. We find Mitelin in the bushes but she won't let us come near her. She is panting hard, her tongue hanging from her mouth that is caked with foam. My sister kneels down and puts out her hand. Mitelin bares her teeth and growls. Her belly heaves violently in and out. She lifts her leg and begins licking the place where Aloysius went in. It is pink and swollen there.

"Mitelin," says my sister, moving closer.

Mitelin snaps her head up and barks.

We back out of the bushes and go into the yard to hunt for fur and blood where Mitelin and Aloysius were.

9

All the Way Under

In the front yard, my sister is stripping one of the forsythia bushes. Already on one side you can see straight through the branches to the ditch. She grabs hold of the top of the branch with both hands and slides her fingers down, pulling off the blossoms until she gets to the end. Then she starts on another branch.

From the porch I call out to her, but she pretends not to hear. She got caught going to the creek and has to stay in the yard. I don't go to the creek anymore. Boys are there. They grab girls and throw them in the water. When my sister came home soaking wet, our father made her strip on the porch. When all her clothes were off, he threw them into the yard and then he went inside the house. She didn't try to hide herself. She saw me watching from the bushes and told me to pick up her clothes from the yard and bring them to her.

I walk down to where my sister is kicking all the pinched-off blossoms into a pile. I pick some up and carry them down to the ditch and scatter them around so it looks like the wind blew them there.

When I get back to the forsythia, my sister is kicking the pile apart. By mistake she kicks me. She kicks me again. It isn't a mistake.

"Quit it," I tell her.

"These are mine," she says.

I don't ask my sister which one of the boys threw her in the water. It might have been Frankie Blackmore or Duane Shields. Duane stays with his cousins who live across the street from us because his family is too poor to keep him. He has blond hair that sticks up straight out of his head and he reads comic books that his cousins keep in stacks in the basement. My sister goes down there to read. I never go.

Now my sister is trying to whip me with a forsythia branch, snapping it near my legs. The whips hurt even though the branch is thin.

"I'll go with you to the creek," I say, to get her to stop whipping the branch at me.

"Come on," she says, flinging the branch into the air.

She takes off across the yard and I run after her. Already my heart is beating fast. We pass by Lily's hiding place in the peonies and then we leave the yard that is crisscrossed with shadows and head for the path to the creek. Ahead of me my sister's bright blond ponytail is flying.

There are no boys around when we get to the creek. We stand on the big flat rocks watching the water pool and spin as it moves through the woods. Light is coming down through the tops of the trees. It is on the rocks and the water, not moving, brightening the air, making our skin glow fiery pink. My sister spits into the water and her spit curls away. I spit but it flies back on me and my sister laughs. I punch her on the arm and she grabs me and shakes me hard, trying to push me in. I push back, but she's stronger. She shoves me again and my foot slips into the water.

After that we both sit down on the rocks. While we're sitting, boys appear at the head of the path. I watch my sister to see what she will do. The boys start coming toward us, with their shirts off sticking out of the waist-bands of their shorts. One of them is Duane Shields and another one is Frankie. He and my sister used to go into the bushes together and put red lipstick on their bodies like gashes.

My sister tells me to stand up. She does this without taking her eyes off the boys, who are getting closer. By the time I stand up, Duane and Frankie have grabbed my sister and are pulling her across the rocks. She is hitting and kicking at them but they have her and she can't twist away. I run into the creek where the water comes up to the tops of my thighs. Instead of coming after me the other boys run to where Frankie and Duane are dangling my sister out over the water, farther down where the current goes under, where once I saw a black snake drop from the branch of a tree into the foaming yellow water.

The boys swing my sister by her arms and legs, counting to three before they heave her into the middle of the creek where the water is fast and deep. She goes all the way under and when her head comes up, she is down to where the water pools again before it drops into another pool far below. I start running toward her in the water, but the rocks are slippery and I keep falling in. The boys hoot and clap from the banks, their voices jumping over the water and the rocks.

One of them says, "Look! She keeps throwing herself in."

Another one says, "Yeah. Trying to get our attention."

A third boy says, "I'd come save you if you had something to save."

They hoot and clap some more. Then they move away from the banks, back into the woods where the tops of their heads disappear in the low branches.

After their voices fade away, I climb out of the water and sit where the sun is coming down through the tops of the trees. My shorts are stuck to my thighs, which make a straight line to my hips. The hair on my calves looks like spider legs.

In the brown sunlight, holding my sides, feeling with my fingertips the bony cage of my ribs, I wait for my sister. The boys are nowhere around. Then I see her, climbing up out of the tumbling water, her clothes sticking to her in the places where she is getting a shape.

"Why didn't you help me?" she says, pushing at me before sitting down on a rock where the sun has moved. Her pinks show through her pale yellow shirt. She flicks her ponytail with her hand, playing with the weight of it.

"I didn't feel like it," I say.

"I could have drowned!"

"The boys would have saved you."

"They'd throw me back in!"

"You like it."

My sister flicks mud at me from the end of a stick she has been poking in the ground. Mud lands on the front of my shirt and in my hair.

I put my hands out in front of me, but she keeps flicking dirt.

"You're just jealous," she says.

"No I'm not."

"I'll tell Frankie and Duane you want them to throw you in."

I get up and run at my sister, punching her hard on the

shoulder. I go for her again and she grabs my wrists and twists my arms until I am down on my knees. I try to kick her but she jumps back, still holding me by my wrists.

"Let go," I tell her.

"No punching," she says.

"Okay."

She lets go and I push at her again, but she jumps away and runs for the path back up to the neighborhood.

I yell at her to wait but she disappears into the woods, her blond ponytail flying past the branches.

My sister is up in the mimosa tree, pulling apart the sticky pink blossoms and throwing them on the ground. I am walking with Mitelin down in the ditch. Every few feet, she stops to sniff at something—a leaf, a piece of burnt plastic, a daddy longlegs. We are not allowed to leave the yard for the rest of the summer. The boys know this and they come by and shout to my sister up in the tree but she pretends not to hear them. They come back but she keeps acting like they're not there.

When Frankie sees me down in the ditch, he grabs Duane by the shoulder and whispers something to him. I take off up the ditch to where the drainpipe runs under the driveway. I crawl in on my hands and knees until I get to the middle. Mitelin thinks it is a game and runs to the other end, where she crawls in to meet me. In the pipe are Mitelin's chew bones, pieces of trash, and the arms and legs and heads of dolls we've tortured.

Duane and Frankie call to me from the end of the drainpipe.

"You have a nice ass, for a ten-year-old," says Frankie, who is thirteen.

Duane says, "Why don't you come over to the basement so we can read some comic books together. Some dirty comics."

They both laugh and then their heads disappear from the end of the drainpipe.

Later, even though my sister shouts that it's safe to come out, I stay in the drainpipe. The blackened rubber bodies of the dolls we used to play with are scattered all around. Mitelin chews on one until I reach up and take it from her.

"Come out!" my sister shouts.

"I'm coming!" I shout back, but first I fling the chewed-up doll ahead of me into the sunburnt grass.

invisible

From the apple tree, I watch Lily moving in the tall grass. She stops when my mother comes out of the house carrying the laundry basket full of clothes. The pockets in the front of my mother's apron bulge with new clothespins. The old ones on the clothesline are black from the sun and the rain. It is very hot and my mother's hair is pulled into a French twist pinned at the back of her head with a long gold comb. Whenever she turns, the comb catches the sunlight. She lifts a blue towel out of the basket and drapes it over the line. Mitelin watches from beneath the wooden porch stairs, her head resting on the bottom slat.

When she gets to the end of the clothesline, my mother picks up the empty basket and holds it against her hip. She stares at the ground where it slopes up to the garden, where once my sister and I asked her to do the hula. She put down the peonies she was carrying in from the yard and broke off one to tuck behind her ear. She put her arms out to one side and began slowly to shimmy her hips until her whole body was vibrating gently like a hummingbird or a moth. She kept doing the dance, in the sunlight in the garden, while Mitelin and Max came up from the ditch and sniffed at her and at the peonies she had laid on the ground. My sister made Mitelin and Max sit and watch, and afterwards, when our mother had gone inside the house, we dog-danced with Mitelin and Max until the dogs got tired of dancing on their hind legs.

Now Mitelin crawls out from under the porch stairs and rubs her muzzle into my mother's free hand. After my mother pets her, Mitelin crawls back under the stairs where it is dark and cool. Lily has disappeared from the tall grass into the bushes.

My mother carries the empty basket to the back porch and sits down. I lean against the tree where I am deep in the leafy shade, invisible.

10

The Sky at Night

At night my sister and I sneak out of the house. We're going to Lilac Hill, which my sister calls Make-Out Hill because that's what everyone does there. We're already dressed and carry our shoes down the stairs. I follow my sister. She knows where to step so we won't make noise.

In the backyard, Mitelin comes over to us, dragging her runner behind her. My sister makes her sit.

"Come on," my sister tells me.

At the mimosa tree in the front yard, my sister stops. Ahead of us the road is inky black. We walk down the hill and push by the forsythia. Past the ditch, my sister stops again.

"Are you afraid?" I ask her.

"What of?" she says.

She starts walking then stops again. It feels like there are boys all around but I don't see any. I tell my sister

that if any boys come near us, I'll run, and she tells me
Go ahead. I'm afraid that if boys come near us, we'll get
pregnant. When I tell this to my sister she turns around
to face me, her hands on her hips, and says, "It doesn't
happen just from being around them." She takes her
hands off her hips and looks around, daring any boys to
come out of the dark.

I want to ask my sister if it's the same as when
Aloysius climbs on Mitelin in the backyard. All I can
think of is being grabbed and pushed to the ground and
not being able to breathe. We keep walking, past where
Mr. Graff the electrician lives, and Colonel and Mrs.
Roberts and Mrs. Shields the cross-walk monitor whose
nephew Duane my sister has a crush on.

"Are you meeting Duane?" I ask her.

She doesn't answer, which means she is.

"Do you like him?" I ask.

"He's sexy," she says.

My face and chest feel hot but I keep following my
sister. We turn onto the road that takes us to Lilac Hill.
I have never been there at night. I keep following my
sister back along the road until we get to the clearing at
the foot of the hill. At the top are two boys. My mouth
fills with water and it feels like I am going to be sick.

"Come on," says my sister and she starts up the hill. I
turn around to leave. The darkness stops me and I run to
catch up with her.

As we get closer to the top, I can see that both boys have their arms crossed and their feet set wide apart. They aren't moving. One is Duane Shields. I don't know who the other one is.

My sister is way ahead of me. When she gets to the top, Duane Shields moves close to her.

The other boy watches me walk the rest of the way up the hill. He has black hair and black eyes. My sister goes off into the dark with Duane Shields. When I reach the top of the hill, the boy I've never seen before comes toward me.

"Who are you?" he says.

I turn and run as fast as I can down Lilac Hill. Even after I make it to the bottom I keep running like there is no end to the night.

My sister has a brown mark on her neck that she is trying to hide by turning up the collar of her shirt. The mark still shows, so she changes into a different shirt, a turtleneck.

"I saw it," I tell her.

"So," she says. She is standing in front of her dresser mirror, making sure the turtleneck completely covers her neck.

"What does it feel like?" I ask.

"Like nothing," she says.

"Does it hurt?"

"No."

"Can I touch it?"

"Leave me alone," she says. Then she tells me to get out of the room. I tell her I don't have to because I was here first. It's one of our rules.

"Then shut up and be quiet," she says. She is brushing her hair, hard, making the ends snap with electricity.

"You can't make me," I say.

She turns around fast with her hairbrush raised up in her hand like she is going to hit me. I put my hands up and cover my head but nothing happens.

"You're a baby," she says. She is standing over me, pulling the hairs out of her hairbrush into clumps and dropping them on me. I throw them back at her but she jumps out of the way. The nests of hair fall to the floor and she kicks them under the bed.

"That's you," she says.

"It's you," I say.

"It's what you look like inside," she says.

"It's what you look like outside."

This time she flings the hairbrush at me and it hits the side of my head. It feels the same as an iceball and I stand up to punch her but she runs out of the room. I pick up the brush and throw it at her dresser mirror, cracking it. From the doorway, I hear her say she's going to tell.

"I don't care," I say. Now the side of my head is

burning hot. A lump is growing there, maybe cancer. I lie down on the bed.

My sister comes into the room and walks over to her dresser to look at the mirror.

"You wrecked it," she says.

"You did," I say back.

She is on top of me again, punching me with her fists, pinning me on the bed. I rear up and push her off. She comes after me again, punching me on the back. Then she moves away.

"You're still a baby," she says.

"A hickey doesn't mean you're grown-up," I say.

"Yes it does," says my sister. She's smiling.

She gets up from the bed and walks back over to her dresser. She starts brushing her hair again, trying it in pigtails, then a braid, then a ponytail which she ties with a red ribbon.

I stay on my bed watching her, feeling over and over with my fingers the place on the side of my head where the hairbrush landed, watching my sister roll down the top of her turtleneck to look at the hickey the color of the sky at night, touching it like it's hers to keep.

bad influence

My mother is sitting in the backyard with Doris Palmer. Mrs. Palmer used to be married to Dick Palmer. Now she is divorced. She is on her way home from the hospital and is still wearing her white nurse's cap stuck on with bobby pins. Underneath the cap is her fire-engine-red hair that comes out of a bottle. My mother's ginger-colored hair has new white-blond streaks, one of Mrs. Palmer's ideas. She also taught my mother how to smoke, and the smoke from their cigarettes is drifting up to the bedroom window where I wait to breathe it in.

Mrs. Palmer won't come to our house if our father is here. That's because he yelled at her for being a bad influence on my mother. The way he yells at boys who come into our yard for being a bad influence on my sister. She goes with boys to Mrs. Shields basement when Mrs. Shields isn't home. In the basement are comic books and her nephew Duane's drum set and some old couches. My sister won't tell me what she does down there, but this summer I found her underpants stuffed into the pocket of the cutoffs she wore over there. When I showed them to her, she pretended they were mine instead of hers. She grabbed them away and threw them on my bed and I threw them back on hers. She took them off her bed and threw them on the floor, where they stayed, getting kicked around until today they were gone. I went outside to where my sister was kneeling and brushing Mitelin with the dog brush and asked her where the underpants were. Without stopping brushing Mitelin's coat, she told me she gave them to Frankie Blackmore as a present from me. I jumped on my sister's back but she bent way over and threw me off. I got up to sock her. Then Frankie Blackmore came into our yard and I ran.

Frankie found me in the bushes and I told him the underpants were my sister's. He pulled them out of his pants pocket and sniffed them and said he knew they couldn't be mine because they smelled like they belonged to a bigger girl. I told Frankie to shut up and then Frankie asked me if I was going to Mrs. Shields and I said never. He left the bushes and found my sister and she went with him. I came out of the bushes and found Mitelin's dog brush in the grass and brushed her coat so hard she yelped.

Now Mrs. Palmer is telling our mother to leave our father, which she always says. But this time she says she'll make some phone calls and then she uses the word "crazy." My mother watches Mrs. Palmer as she talks, her eyes blinking in the bright sunlight.

The two women sit with their legs crossed and their iced-tea glasses set on the wide flat arms of the wooden sun chairs. Every once in a while as they talk, Mrs. Palmer looks in the direction of the driveway to see if our father is coming.

My mother finishes her cigarette and puts it out in the grass. Mrs. Palmer keeps smoking hers, all the way down past the filter, and then sticks it under her thick white shoe. When Mrs. Palmer talks, she makes everything sound like it is easy, and when my mother talks, everything sounds like it is hard.

Before she leaves, Mrs. Palmer gives my mother a quick hug. She is fast and full of energy, which is not at all like my mother. Sometimes it is hard to tell if my mother is doing anything at all.

Mrs. Palmer walks quickly down to the driveway and then I hear her get into her car and drive away. My mother puts her head down and her shoulders drop forward, the way they used to when she would show us the shimmy. She starts to cry, a strangled-off sound without any tears.

She stops crying after a minute or two and goes inside the house, stopping on the steps of the back porch to light a cigarette. The match hisses into the grass.

I think about going outside and drinking from their iced-tea glasses. Instead I just lie down on my bed. The sheets are cool and I stare up at the ceiling at nothing. I hear my mother come up the stairs and go into the bedroom and close the door. She starts to cry, and this time it sounds like she isn't going to stop.

At first I'm mad at Mrs. Palmer for telling my mother she should leave. It's like boys telling you to do things you don't want to. I change my mind. I don't think Mrs. Palmer is a bad influence after all, not like boys are. If you don't do what boys want, they can make you do it anyway.

When my mother finally stops crying, the sun is going down and the room is full of golden light. I look around at all my things which I know by heart and then I close my eyes. All I see is stupid Frankie Blackmore sniffing my sister's underpants in the bushes.

My sister comes in and I tell her about our mother and Mrs. Palmer. She walks over to the window and looks down into the backyard like they are still sitting there. Then she walks down the hall to our mother and father's room.

In a few minutes, my sister comes back.

"We're not leaving," she says and then she goes into the closet where we change clothes when we don't want the other person watching.

When she doesn't come out, I go and listen at the door. It sounds like she's crying. I walk back over to my bed and lie down.

Looking up at the light on the ceiling that is already starting to fade, I change my mind again about Mrs. Palmer. I think she is a bad influence, not because she taught our mother how to smoke and dye her hair or because she wants her to leave our father. It's not like she's a boy who can make you do things. I think Mrs. Palmer is a bad influence because she makes leaving seem like it is easy.

My sister comes out of the closet and I pretend to be asleep. With my eyes closed I keep seeing Frankie, but that isn't the hard part. The hard part is not crying until my sister leaves the room.

11

Pinks

All week my sister and I climb up into the mimosa tree to watch for the chain gang coming down the road. They are patching the street with tar, which they spread from a black vat that rolls on wheels behind them. The men tending the vat have their shirts off. Their chests look bone-white in the bright sunlight. The others bend low to the road, stretching their arms and necks out over their long shadows. Two policemen wearing sunglasses and hats stand in the ditches on either side of the street, aiming their rifles at the prisoners. None of the men are talking, so we listen to the sound of their rakes and shovels and hoes. The chains around their ankles are the same color as the guns. They glimmer and shake whenever one of the prisoners takes a step.

"Which one do you like?" my sister asks me.

I look at all the men and at the heat coming up in

waves around them shimmying off the wet tar. I pick the one with a lean face and jet-black eyes who is wearing a gold cross around his neck. When he bends over to smooth the tar, the crucifix swings out in an arc from his chest.

"That one," I tell my sister. I show her by pointing.

"Mine is next to the barricade," she says. "The one with the tattoo."

Hers is handsome in a young way. Mine is good-looking, too, but his face is more manly.

"I bet yours is a murderer," my sister says.

We watch the convicts. Their hair is shaved close to their scalps. It makes their heads look like they are glowing. I take a deep breath of the tar and hold it in until it feels like I am going to pass out.

My sister's legs dangle from the branch above me. The sunlight makes the hair on her calves look golden.

"It might take them a while to get to our house," I tell her.

"You watch then," she says. "I'm going in."

After she has climbed down, I hold on to the branch above me and lean out as far as I can from the tree. All I can see is the grass under the tree that is smashed flat where my sister and I took turns jumping earlier. The other place we jump from is the roof of the garage. We climb the mulberry tree to the roof and then drop down into the pen our father built with nothing in it. In the summer it is too hot to sit on the unshaded side, so we hang back beneath the branches. The mulberries are white and soft like the bodies of the white spiders that nest under the porch stairs. Mitelin had her puppies under there.

The policemen shout back and forth across the road and I look up as the convicts start to move. Most of them keep their heads bowed as they walk, watching their feet. When they are almost in front of our house, the police-men raise their guns for them to stop. I climb down out of the mimosa tree and run around the house to the garage. From the roof, I can see the men even closer, shoveling gravel onto the road. My sister calls to me through the screen in our bedroom window.

"Are they doing anything?"

"Just working," I tell her.

She moves away from the window and puts on her tap-dancing music. She's only allowed to practice when our father isn't home. I hear her dancing on top of the flattened cardboard box that she keeps under her bed.

I stay up on the roof. The smell of tar is in my hair and clothes. It hangs in the air. I watch my convict for a while. His back is long and thin like his face. It is too narrow for the pony rides our father used to give us when he was in a good mood. We'd have to grab onto his shirt at his neck or he'd buck us off. My convict turns around and I duck down. While I am waiting to sit back up, my father's car pulls into the driveway.

I lie flat against the roof, still as a stick. My sister snaps off the record player in our room. The car comes all the way up the driveway and I can see the top of my father's sun-shield hat when he gets out. Something is lying in the backseat. At first I think it's a man, but when it moves I see that it's a sheep tied down with rope.

My father opens the back door and pulls the sheep bucking and twisting out of the backseat. He kicks the door shut and then carries the sheep upside down to the pen, where he unties it. At first the sheep doesn't move but then it struggles up, its back legs kicking as it moves off toward the tall grass and flowering weeds at the back of the pen. My father watches the sheep for a while and then he lets himself out of the pen. I lie on the roof until my father goes into the house. The sheep chews off the tops of the tall grass. Its wool is light brown and around its muzzle and near its eyes it is dark brown.

I call to the sheep, but it keeps eating the grass. I jump down into the pen and stand apart from it until it is used to me. Then I walk slowly toward it with my hands facing palm out.

From the roof of the garage, I watch my convict. The sun shines on his back and on the blacktop where he and the others have tarred. I shut my eyes tight and his image appears, burning through my eyelids bright red then black. When I open my eyes again, my convict is even closer, throwing down shovelfuls of tar and gravel on a patch of road in front of our driveway. The muscles in his chest and neck and arms stand out shining with sweat when he flings the tar and gravel onto the road.

The kitchen door slams and my sister comes out of the house, her ponytail switching from side to side as she walks. My hair is pulled back from my face with a white bandeau that I fastened with two bobby pins. My convict doesn't know I am wearing my hair this way for him.

I stand up and walk to the edge of the roof overlooking the pen. The sheep is backed up to the fence, chewing. I sit down and wait for my sister.

"He doesn't have a name," I tell her after she has climbed up onto the roof.

"How do you know it's a male?" she says.

"I don't."

"See if there's any part hanging down."

I lean out to look at the sheep under there but all I can see is wool.

"We'll look later," says my sister. "First we have to name it."

"How about Smokey," I say.

"Too stupid," says my sister.

"I know," she says, looking at the sheep. "We'll call it Lee Henry, after my convict."

"How do you know his name?" I walk over to where she's standing.

"I asked," she says.

"How could you. We're not allowed to talk to them."

"Well I did."

She stands up and walks with her hands on her hips to the front of the roof. I can tell she is watching her convict because her head is very still and her hips are locked the way they do when she is concentrating.

"What if he tried to kiss you," I say.

"I'd let him," she says without turning around.

I think about my convict, what his name might be, what it would be like to kiss him.

"Yours might try to strangle you," my sister says.

Some of the convicts look up at the garage from their work, but the policemen raise their rifles.

My sister walks to the edge of the roof and calls down to the sheep. "Lee Henry," she says in a singsong voice. "Lee Henry." Lee Henry keeps chewing the tall grass.

The kitchen door slams and my father comes out. We get down low to the roof. He has on his sun-shield hat. He isn't wearing a shirt. His scapula is tangled in the curly black hair on his chest. The hair is on his back and his arms. At his waist, holding up his pants, is the rope he used to tie Lee Henry's legs.

He walks across the yard and gets into the pen. He pokes at Lee Henry with the fire stick he keeps at the back of the garage. Lee Henry moves away from him, following the fence around and around. My father puts the stick down and walks over to Lee Henry. He grabs him by his muzzle and turns it from side to side. When he lets go, Lee Henry rocks his head violently like Michael Knight down the street who is epileptic.

After my father leaves the pen, we climb back up and sit on the peak of the roof. There is more light at the bottom of the sky now than at the top. The smoke from the flare pots that the prisoners are setting out is oily black. It blows sideways out of the openings and curls around the prisoners' legs. Some of the men cough and wave the smoke away. Mine looks like he has tears in his eyes.

My sister says, "Yours is crying."

"It's the smoke," I tell her.

"He's crying for you."

I punch her on the shoulder. She punches me back. We stay up on the roof of the garage until the last prisoner gets on the prison bus. My sister waves at the prisoners but all we can see is the backs of their shaved heads. We wait until the bus is at the top of the hill and then we climb down the branches of the mulberry tree and go inside.

At dinner our father tells us our mother has shingles and that we can't see her until he says so. We don't know what shingles are but we don't ask. We don't ask about Lee Henry either. After dinner, I give the rest of my food to Mitelin, who has been waiting under the table. My father goes into the living room to lie down on the couch. Soon he is snoring.

I walk in to where he is sleeping. His head is jammed up against the end of the couch and his mouth is open, a black spiral. I listen to him breathing. His arm goes up over his head and he turns in toward the back of the couch. I watch the metal plate to see if it will catch the light from the lamp on the end table, but he doesn't move and the back of his head stays dark.

My sister calls to me from the side yard. We meet up on the roof of the garage, on the side facing Lee Henry's pen. We can't see him. Tufts of wool are stuck in the bushes and the tall weeds. The evening sun is behind us. It warms the back of my head. I feel for the ends of my hair and then reach for my sister's ponytail. She swings her head away. The sky changes from bright orange to blue-black. My sister catches a firefly and puts it on her shirt.

"Look," she says, holding her shirt out from her chest. The light glows pearl white and then goes out. She flicks the dead bug from her shirt, down into Lee Henry's pen.

I stand up and walk to the edge of the roof. Lee Henry's legs are sticking out from under the holly bush.

The kitchen door slams and my sister signals me to get down. We lie flat against the roof, listening as our father stops by the trash can at the back of the garage. The whites of my sister's eyes are shiny and wet. She puts her finger to her lips for me to not make a sound.

The gate to the pen opens and Lee Henry's legs kick against the garage as he gets up. Now we can see our father, right under us. He moves across the pen with his fire stick raised over his head and brings it down on top of Lee Henry's back. With a grunt my father brings the stick down again, driving it into Lee Henry's head. Electricity travels from my ribs into the part between my legs. It spirals out to my thighs. A taste like vinegar and salt comes into my mouth. My father hits him a third time and Lee Henry falls down. Out of his mouth comes a sound like Mitelin having puppies. The electricity has gone out of me and it feels like I am up in the air like a firefly, like smoke. I reach for my sister but she's gone.

Our father grabs Lee Henry by the legs and drags him out of the pen. He takes him up the hill to the wire trash can and after that I smell wool and gasoline and grass and fire and smoke.

I stay up on the roof, not moving, remembering how stiff Lee Henry's wool felt the first time I touched him, like curly paper. In the pen, he let me hold him around the neck and then he let me climb onto his back. I rode him but after a few steps he bucked me off and I flipped over on my side into the grass.

In the middle of the night my sister wakes me up.

"Come on," she says and we go downstairs and out the back door to Lee Henry's pen. My sister shines a flashlight into the pen, onto the patch of bloody grass where Lee Henry fell.

She lets me hold the flashlight and I shine it around the pen. Pieces of Lee Henry's wool float in the air. Some of it is stuck in the tall weeds and under the holly bush and to the side of the garage. My sister grabs the flashlight away and shuts it off.

I follow her up the hill to the wire trash can. In the dark we can see the spills of white ash. My sister turns on the flashlight and walks slowly around the trash can. She tells me to find a stick and when I do she takes it and pokes it at the chunks of ash. I wait until she is done and then I poke the stick way in until it comes out the other side. Something inside of me slides upwards and I vomit.

"Come on," my sister says, yanking the stick away. She hurls it over the fence into our neighbor's yard.

I don't move.

"Come on!" she yells.

I still don't move. My sister shakes me. Then she grabs my hand and pulls me down the hill.

The chain gang has moved past our house to where the street gets hilly again. My sister and I climb up into the mimosa tree to watch them.

"Where's yours?" my sister says.

"Maybe he's sick today," I say when I can't find him.

"Maybe they sent him to the chair," my sister says, like she knows.

That feeling goes through me, starting in my ribs and spreading down. I picture my convict slumped in the electric chair, his head hanging, his hands bound. When the guard lifts his head to make sure he is dead, my convict is still handsome, like the picture of the prince with jet-black hair I keep locked in my jewelry box.

"Do you think they tortured him first?" I ask my sister.

"Sure," she says. "They always do."

It is a hot day. We climb out of the mimosa tree and walk to the apple tree in the backyard, which has more shade. Lily looks up from where she is eating grass at the top of the hill, then puts her head back down.

Up in the branches, we start our torture session. My sister unbuttons her shirt. When she moves I can see her nipples. We call them our pinks, deep pink in the middle surrounded by light pink. While I unbutton my shirt, she grabs onto the nearest branch and swings down. She moves out along the branch, making room for me to swing down next to her.

We hang from the branch, our bodies slack. The palms of my hands burn into the wood. My sister begins to writhe, twisting her body slowly back and forth.

"No," she moans. "No, no, no."

I drop my head and start to moan.

"Use your body," my sister tells me.

I twist around, arching my back until it feels like there are needles sticking into my ribs.

"Now they're going to whip us," she says.

Her body jerks violently. Her eyes are closed and her face is pinched with pain.

"Are you doing it?" she asks me.

"Yes," I say, and I grind my body in the air, faster and faster until I hear her drop and then I drop down beside her. We lie there without moving and then slowly my sister lifts her head. Her blond hair shines.

"Were you naked?" she asks me.

"I still am."

A breeze moves across my body.

"Look," I say.

We watch my pinks harden and rise.

jump

From the blue hydrangea, we watch our father down in the ditch. He is burning off piles of tall grass and weeds from the pen where Lee Henry died. My sister says our father is a murderer for killing Lee Henry and that if we ever tell, he could get the electric chair. So far we haven't told anyone, not even our mother.

He keeps moving along the ditch, poking his fire stick at the smoking heaps. Even though the sun is out, he isn't wearing his sun-shield hat. When he turns and walks back down the length of the ditch, light streaks from the metal plate at the back of his head. His black scapula flips and twists in the breeze.

Mitelin comes out from under the forsythia where she has been sleeping and sniffs at the fires, jumping back and forth across the ditch until she finds a place where she can get close to the flames and then backing away from the heat and smoke. Our father walks and walks, prodding the flames with his long stick, turning the heaps of weeds over to keep the flames burning high. Ash spins and floats in the air.

Mitelin runs from the ditch up to where we are hiding in the bushes. My sister tells her to get away but she comes into the bushes and sits with us. The breeze stops and the smoke spreads out, covering our father in a thick cloud.

"He's gone," I say.

"He's there," says my sister.

The breeze picks up, clearing the smoke, and our father is there, moving along the ditch, turning and turning the ash-black heaps with his stick.

After a while, my sister and I crawl out from under the hydrangea bushes and run to the garage. We climb up the mulberry tree and onto the roof so we can jump down into the pen. The one who jumps first gets to make the other one jump onto the spot where Lee Henry died. Our father has covered it over with mulch from the garden, where nothing is growing. The rest of the grass is burnt yellow from the sun. So far, my sister has always jumped first.

We are both ready at the edge of the roof. This time I let go. When I hit the ground, my sister tells me I cheated by letting go before she was ready. She says my jump doesn't count. But I stand up and yell at her to jump. "Come and make me," she says. I run around the garage to the mulberry tree, but when I get to the roof, my sister is gone. She isn't in the pen.

I sit down at the edge of the roof, holding on, and

then I make the jump, down onto the flat brown circle of mulch where Lee Henry died. I keep doing this until it is past dark and my sister finds me with a flashlight. She shines it up at the roof of the garage while I make the jump and then she shines it down in my face and says, You're going crazy, just like Dad. She says if our mother doesn't do something she's going to run away, Even from you, she says, clicking off the flashlight. Get up, she tells me and then she leaves the pen.

12

The Last Place

Inside, our father and mother are arguing. At first, my sister and I listen on the back porch. We hear yelling and then we hear our father hitting his head against the wall. My sister says it means our mother knows about Lee Henry, but I don't think she found out, unless my sister told her. When I ask her if she told, my sister says I am a jerk and to shut up. After that we stay quiet, listening to their voices and watching for any furniture coming out the windows.

Now we're under the apple tree where the air is cool and dark. Mitelin is with us, asleep on her side in the thick grass. Flies hop-fly around her face and belly. She is going to have puppies again and even though her belly is flat, her teats are starting to darken and swell. I stroke the part leading down to her leg that is smooth and soft. Some of the hair comes off in my hand. When I wiggle my fingers, the hair floats in the air, barely moving.

After a while the house gets quiet and I stare at the red bricks and at the curtains being sucked out the windows by the breeze.

Mitelin shifts in her sleep. Next to her, my sister lies with her eyes closed, her legs bent at her knees. I can see where her shorts end, way up at the top of her thighs. Her hands are crossed on her stomach. She used to fold her arms on her chest but her friend Deborah McDermott told her not to or her breasts wouldn't grow. I watch the front of her shirt to see if she is breathing. After I turn away, the image of her shirt floats into the air and hangs there.

Our mother comes out the back door with a suitcase and carries it down the driveway to her car. She puts the suitcase in the trunk and then leans against it, with her head down and her arms crossed on her chest. After a few minutes, she goes back inside the house. I tell my sister to get up because our mother is packing the car.

"Mrs. Cooley's," says my sister, but she gets up anyway and Mitelin and I follow her out front to the driveway. My sister tries to open the trunk of our mother's car but it's locked. She takes a step back and kicks the car with her foot. Mitelin barks.

"What are you doing?" I ask her.

"What does it look like?" she says, kicking the car again. Mitelin keeps barking.

I tell my sister to stop because our mother is coming out of the house with another suitcase. Behind her is our father and his angry blue eyes are on her. He grabs our mother's suitcase and throws it in the bushes. Then he pushes by her and yells at us to get into his car. My sister tells me not to move and grabs Mitelin by her choke collar and makes her sit. We don't move and he comes at us, picking us up by our arms. Everything goes sideways and I hear Mitelin barking and then I see my father's foot kicking Mitelin away as he pushes us into his car.

Our father gets into the front seat and starts the engine. Then he takes his gun from the glove compartment and points it out the window at our mother, who keeps moving toward the car. I scream and my sister grabs me by my head and pulls me down onto the seat. The car rolls backwards and when we are almost at the bottom of the driveway, my sister opens the door on her side and jumps out, running for the bushes.

I'm afraid to make the jump. Then my sister screams my name and I move toward the door, away from my father's arm reaching back across the top of the seat. I jump and the ground comes up at me. The bushes and the trees roll away and then the drainpipe at the bottom of the driveway curves toward me and I crawl in. Lily is hunched down inside but she runs out when our father's car rumbles overhead. The gun goes off and the car races to the top of the hill and then it is quiet.

I stay down in the drainpipe until I hear my sister call from the forsythia bushes and then I crawl out and run to her, not even feeling the slaps of the long slender branches.

We are upstairs packing but we're not going to Mrs. Cooley's, which is the only other place we've been. Our mother said to pack our beach towels and bathing suits and zories because we're going to the beach. I ask my sister where the beach is and she says Next to the water, where do you think. Our mother also told us to bring heavy clothes like pullovers and corduroy pants. Now my sister is packing her Chubby Checker and Beatles records and her chemistry set.

"Bring a lot," she tells me. "We're not coming back."

"Mom said a week."

"Then leave all your stuff here," she says, putting her books and her pom-poms and the bullet box into her suitcase. There is hardly any room left.

Even though I don't believe her, I look around the room to see what I should take. There's my rock collection and Chopin record and the naked paper dolls in the heart-shaped box. Now she's putting in her poodle drawings and her holy-water angel.

"What about Dad?" I ask her.

"What about him?" she says.

She sits down on her bed and rips off her play shirt and throws it on the floor. She's supposed to wear a bra every day but sometimes when it's too hot she doesn't, like today. Her pinks are dark now, not like mine, which still are pale. She puts on a new shirt but then she rips it off and puts on another one.

I sit on my bed, picturing the hole in my father's head, that black space covered over with a shiny metal plate. Our mother says he won't come back this time. My sister says he could come back any minute. I don't say anything about outer space.

My sister waves her hand in front of my face.

"Yoo hoo?" she says.

I stand up and pack some more of my things. I think about the beach, wondering what the waves will be like, whether we will be able to hear the ocean at night. My sister says you can find things on the sand like smooth pieces of glass and old china and seashells in the shape of tornadoes. Still, it's hard to picture a place where there are no trees or grass or bushes, only sand and wind and water.

When we've finished packing, we drag our suitcases down the stairs. I have to struggle with mine because it's full of rocks. We're taking Mitelin but not Lily because she ran away. My sister says she probably got eaten by a crow or a fox. I think she's hiding in the blackberry bushes past our yard, even though we went searching and didn't find her. At night I look out our bedroom window for Lily. There is only the apple tree and the fence around the sump pump and Mitelin's chain hanging from the clothesline.

Outside, on the porch, we put down our suitcases and rest. It is a hot day. The sun shines on our arms and legs and on the metal locks of the suitcases. It shines on the steps leading down to the bright grass and on the leaves of the mimosa tree that tremble even when there is no wind and on the sticky pink blossoms that are turning pale brown where they have fallen on the ground. It shines on the forsythia bush where Mitelin is lying fast asleep in her scooped-out spot.

Past the forsythia the ditch lies black, smelling of smoke and ash.

"Come on," says my sister, and she drags her suitcase down the steps. I turn my suitcase on its side and yank it down one step at a time, then follow my sister to the driveway.

We wait by the burned-up car propped on cinder blocks, where our mother told us to be when she gets back from the gas station. We already found the bullet hole in the windshield from the day our father tried to kidnap us. We counted all the lines spidering out from the hole, and we each put our pinky fingers through the hole twice without touching it.

My sister says she is bored and walks to the dogwood

tree. She pulls on the branches to see how far she can lean back without snapping any off.

I walk down to the century plants at the bottom of the driveway. Most of the time, the plants look dead, but during the summer they turn green and sometimes they flower. The flowers last about a week and then they drop off. Usually they fall down inside the leafy bases of the plants where you can't get at them because of the prickers. This summer I put my hand inside and dozens of needles stuck to my fingers and wrist. My sister had to use our mother's eyebrow tweezers to pull them out. Afterwards, the back of my hand was covered with tiny red welts. I squeezed one and a clear liquid came out. My sister said a flower would grow from my hand there, but so far one hasn't.

Now the stalks shoot up out of the base of the plants like missiles, like Lily's leg when she lifted it to lick the part where her tail used to be. Lily might come back. I call to my sister to ask again if Lily will come back and she lets go of the branches of the dogwood tree, lets them fly back up, and says, "No way."

Our mother's car pulls into the driveway and we run for our suitcases. She helps us put the suitcases up front under the hood and then she leans against the car and lights a cigarette. She tells us to find Mitelin and put her in the car and when we get back our mother is still smoking the cigarette, down past the filter like Mrs. Palmer.

My sister tells me to get Mitelin's water dish and chew bones from the backyard. Near the apple tree where the chew bones are scattered it looks like someone is coming toward me but it's the shadow of a branch darkening the grass.

When I get back to the car, my sister opens the door on her side and I push by her into the backseat. Mitelin gets one of the chew bones in her mouth and jumps into the well with it. All the windows are rolled down but it is still hot inside the car. Our mother starts the engine and lifts her foot off the brake and slowly we roll backwards down the driveway.

Mitelin drops her chew bone and looks out the back window and I tell her we're going on a trip to the beach.

"She wouldn't know," says my sister.

"She might," I say.

"Dummy."

"You are."

"Girls," says my mother.

My mother has put on her dark glasses. My sister is wearing her dark glasses, too, even though one of the stems is missing. I sit back in my seat as my mother brings the car to a stop at the bottom of the driveway.

Instead of backing out onto the street, she puts the car

in neutral. My sister looks up at her but doesn't say anything. We sit stopped at the bottom of the driveway, over the drainpipe where I last hid, and I remember hearing the gravel fly out from under the tires of my father's car, the stones hitting the top of the metal drainpipe and the undersides of the car, and then I remember the gun going off, thinking the bullet was going to hit me or my mother or my sister or Mitelin or Lily. That's when I understand that my sister is right. We're not coming back. And neither is Jupiter or Lily or Lee Henry or the mother cat or her dead daughter.

I try to push past my sister in the front seat and run to the mimosa tree and the mulberry tree and to the blackberry bushes past the woodpile at the back of our yard. My sister jams her body against the back of the seat and stops me.

To my mother she says, "You can go," and my mother backs the car onto the street. I sit back and Mitelin's head, hanging over the top of the seat from the well, knocks into mine.

Out my window, up the slope of the front yard past the forsythia and the crepe myrtle and the blue hydrangea, is the house. The red bricks shimmer in the heat, and then the car starts forward and the house is gone.

hill

At the top of the hill, our father passes us in his car. He's wearing his gorilla mask and holding on to the steering wheel with his hairy rubber hands. He doesn't see us and keeps driving down the street toward our house.

Epilogue:
The Real Hawaii

By the pool at the Waikiki, my sister says our father will never find us. I don't believe her. There are hardly any good places to hide here, I tell her, especially outside. She says if he comes we'll just run, and then she tell me to shut up. She wants to get back in the water. She dives from the edge into the deep end and doesn't come up for a long time. Under the water, her body moves like a pale, angry snake.

Our mother wears sunglasses and stays in her chaise longue, which she keeps moving into the shade. All the table umbrellas have been painted to look like palm trees and the pool house is covered with fronds to look like a thatched hut. At the restaurant, the hostesses wear leis and grass skirts over their flower-print shifts. Behind their ears are tissue-paper flowers fastened with bobby pins. The waitresses also wear leis, which they sometimes take off and give to the customers. They aren't real leis like the ones my sister and I made for the hula show. They're made of shiny white plastic. So far none of the waitresses has given us one.

Mitelin isn't supposed to stay with us but at night we sneak her up to our room on the second floor. Her toenails clack on the metal staircase and at the top she stops to sniff the wind through the railing. The first night we brought her to the room, we made her sleep in the bathroom in case she barked. In the morning all the water was gone from the toilet bowl, so now she sleeps on the floor between our mother's bed and ours.

Our mother says we might stay at the Waikiki another week. We don't ask why. My sister says she likes it here, that it's the closest we'll ever get to the real Hawaii. At first, she wanted us to put on the hula show, in front of the pool changing rooms that are painted with volcanoes, pineapple groves, dancing hula girls, and hula men playing ukuleles. She said we could borrow leis and grass skirts from the hostesses and charge the guests admission. When I said I wouldn't do the show she started pounding me with her fists by the pool but then she lost her balance and fell in.

The lifeguard made her sit out for half an hour in a chair where he could watch her. Afterward, she said she didn't mind because the lifeguard was cute. I don't think he's cute. His chest is covered with curly brown hair and so are his hands, like our father's when he's a gorilla. My sister says she's going to get the lifeguard to kiss her before we leave. She says things like that, now that she has breasts.

When I get tired of watching her swim underwater, I walk to the shallow end of the pool and step in, past a boy and girl who are playing Marco Polo. I wade in to where the water comes up to my chin and then I push off from the bottom of the pool onto my back, my arms spread straight out from my sides. I stay like that, doing the dead man's float, my whole body light as ash on the surface of the water.

With my eyes closed, I can see our house floating up out of the forsythia and the blue hydrangea. The bricks are liquid, made of colored water, and out the windows the curtains flow like white lava. I don't see our father in the picture, but I know he's there, waiting to find us. He'll look in the bushes and on the roof of the garage, down in the drainpipe, behind the woodpile, up in the mimosa tree, and when we're not in any of those places, he'll come after us with tears in his eyes, just like we never left.